Speedway Thunder

Larry Mellott

Copyright © 2017 Larry Mellott

A Start-Living Homes publication
514 E. Circle Dr. Dover, PA 17315

Printed in the USA

10 9 8 7 6 5 4 3 2

ISBN: 978-0-9824161-1-2
Library of Congress Control Number: 2017913686

www.larrymellott.weebly.com

DEDICATION

To edit it good
so it reads as it should,
my wife gave the time that it took.
She helped with corrections
and made some suggestions
so to her I dedicate this book.

Thank you, Bonnie.

Speedway Thunder

CHAPTER 1

FIFTEEN-YEAR-OLD BRENT LOCKEMAN sat quietly on the outside of the third row of the Conleyville Kart Track starting grid. He sized up the five karts that qualified ahead of him for the Yamaha Sprint class feature race. The pair of Quantums that owned the front row was a brother and sister act equipped with all the latest 'tricks' their 'Go-Lightning' kart shop sponsor could offer. The only unknown factor was which sibling would wave the victory trophy as the family entourage paraded from the pits at the end of the day. Brent banked on snatching at least the third place honors with his aged but strategically reworked mount.

His uncle, Martin Kessick, knelt beside him on the pre-grid awaiting the finish of the modified class that was out on the track. "Get your helmet on and concentrate on a good clean start. Don't let the Branson kids cloud your thinking. Put it behind you."

Brent pulled the helmet over his fluffy blonde hair. "They tag-teamed me with that last lap pinch. I had the groove going up the hill and they knew it."

"It's over," Martin said firmly. The brawny, self-employed home builder knew all too well the frustrations of racing competition. He himself was a former state karting champion. "This is a new race with new situations. Don't focus so much on what's behind you that you lose sight of what's ahead."

Brent's widowed mother, Katherine Lockeman, stood beside them behind the chain-link fence. "Please be careful," she pleaded. "And keep away from those two purple and yellow karts." She made no secret of her apprehension for her son's interest in racing.

A petite Suz Kessick gently comforted her sister-in-law with a hug around the waist. "Brent has always demonstrated good judgment in his racing experience. He's a natural...just like his uncle."

Brent snapped his neck collar in place and pulled on his snug driving gloves. "I was just hoping for a better showing than this since I raced last."

Martin tapped him on the helmet. "That was two years ago, Brent. Every year out of the seat makes you a bit rustier. Heck, imagine what affect the years will have on me." He paused. "Brent, you came from eleventh place to finish sixth with only one practice and one qualifying heat after a two year absence. I'd say you proved yourself pretty good."

Brent huffed. "But I went from first to sixth in half a lap thanks to the conspiracy."

Martin addressed him more sternly. "Hey, there's no room on the track for grudges. Put it behind you. I want to see a clean race."

The last of the throaty, modified Briggs and Strattons exited the track as the PA system crackled to life. "Attention in the pits. Yamaha should be on the pre-grid. Come on Yamahas, this is your race."

The flagman leaned over the side of the elevated flag stand and gave the one minute signal. Engines on all sides blipped to life. Martin inserted the starter shaft into the side of the 100cc 2-cycle engine and spun it over.

Ring-ding-ding. The motorcycle engine fired instantly. Ring-ding-ding. Brent tapped the throttle lightly and crouched deeper into the fiberglass seat.

"Be careful," he read his mother's lips as the flagman waved the group onto the track.

The leading Bransons restricted the field to a slower than usual pace lap, setting the stage to unleash their own dominance at the drop of the green flag. Brent read the maneuver, having seen it unfold many times before. He inched closer to the fourth place kart in the row just ahead of him. But he wished it was the two leaders up in the front row that he was crowding.

No grudges, he reminded himself as he felt a bump from behind.

Rounding Turn 4 and parading up the hill where he was shut out the last time, he gritted his teeth. He watched the two leaders suppress the class through the esses and into Turn 10. "Just two pawns and then you're both mine," he said to himself within the confines of a full face helmet.

He anticipated what happened coming out of Turn 10. The 'Go-Lightning' duo abruptly launched onto the main straightaway toward the green flag and left the entire field in its wake.

Brent had already eased back from the row ahead to create some room for himself and exited the turn under full throttle. When the flag waved he was along the outside pulling even with the two karts in the row ahead.

They blasted down the front straight three abreast. But Brent had the momentum. Crossing the start-finish line he was past them and in third place.

He stayed on the outside edge. The two leaders braked for Turn 1, hogging the inside. Brent used every inch of macadam entering the left turn and delicately tapped his brake. From the outside he dove across the track and hit the apex squarely with his inside tire. Inertia floated him back to the outside as he opened onto the chute toward Turn 2. He was alone, the purple and yellow pair ahead, and the snarling mob behind.

He glided effortlessly through the next fast elbow without even a mere touch on the brake and was with the two leaders when they entered the hard braking Turn 3. They spilled down the hill as triplets, well ahead of the rest of the field.

The Turn 4 hairpin offered no room for advancement. Up the hill and through the esses the leaders wiggled to and fro. Turn 9 had the Branson kids still side by side with Brent tapping their push bars.

Equipped with the most recent exhaust on the market, the latest tire compound available and the newest aerodynamic body panels that existed, it was no surprise the two leaders opened up a gap down the front straight. In fact, their body panels were so new, they weren't even available to the general racing public. Straightaway speed was definitely to their advantage. To get past them, Brent knew he would have to out-corner them.

The gap widened by two kart lengths by Turn 1. The leaders maintained a side-by-side block around the Turn 2 sweeper, down the back stretch and around Turn 3. The most Brent could manage was to nip each of their bumpers to let them know he was there. They ruled the front row masterfully.

A solid blue kart originally in third place announced its presence at the bottom of the hill with a tap to Brent's rear bar, nearly sending him on a spin into the hairpin. Although he saved the pending spin, Brent found himself clawing for traction on the outside edge with a new foe taking command of the inside.

For three laps the quartet fought to hold their positions. Any gain the Branson's achieved on the main straight was surrendered again by Turn 4. With his new unyielding blue challenger riding the rail, Brent was resigned to an inferior groove on the outside. He had to get past his fresh nemesis.

The Branson siblings led the field with the precision of drum majors leading a band in a parade. No wavering from dominion, no deviation from what seemed like a rehearsed beat. By Lap 8, the foursome pulled up on the straggling lone rear kart of the field. Thundering down the main straightaway with no loss in stride, they drifted wide to make the pass. Seeing some room on the left, Brent threw his kart to the inside and launched toward the rail.

The leading Quantums cleared the lapped kart and glided left only to find Brent had slipped into the hole. Smoke poured from the hot tires as frantic braking locked up wheels entering Turn 1. Brent held the small steering wheel firm as the Quantum on his right rammed him at the turn-in point.

Both karts wiggled dizzyingly. Eight tires barked from the impact as the two karts slid wildly into the bend.

The Branson brother/sister act kept the squeeze on to force Brent from their front row stronghold. Shoehorned along the railing, Brent fought to hold his ground. He felt the tag-team conspiracy all over again.

They roared three abreast into the chute with the solid blue kart pressing them from behind.

Brent shot through the sweeper pushing away

from the rail as much as inertia would allow. Fans in the bleachers were on their feet as the warring gladiators dueled into the tight Turn 3.

Brent knew he initiated a challenge he was committed to seeing through. He braked later than usual and relied on his adversary to become his guardrail, his security. He smacked into the purple and yellow side pods on his right but held his line around the screaming, scorching turn.

On the downhill approach to the right-handed hairpin, he was trapped by one Quantum on the outside, unable to cross the track, while the other Quantum and the solid blue challenger waged a battle of their own directly behind.

Expecting a push to the outside from his foe, a payback for his own security maneuver just seconds earlier, Brent tapped his brake pedal. Barely missing his nose cone, the Quantum shot across the track and disappeared off course onto the grass.

Brent stabbed the throttle and hurled the kart across the pavement to the apex where he wanted to be all along. Fully aware of the duo pressing from behind, he cleared the hairpin in first place and blasted up the hill toward the esses.

At the start-finish line the white flag waved overhead. Last lap. Brent slipped smoothly past two more karts before Turn 1 and another one on the backstretch. At the hairpin, the grass run-off area showed evidence of wayward activity but no sign of a stranded Quantum kart.

He exited Turn 10 to a clear track ahead and crossed the finish line one last time for the checkered flag.

Completing the cool down lap, Brent coasted through the pit gate to find a congregation had formed

14

around his own pit. He drifted down pit road and killed the engine in front of Uncle Martin. What appeared to be a heated argument was already in progress.

"You should be black flagged from competition," a shaggy-cut, black haired teenager screamed at Brent. "You banged me the whole race till you finally rammed me off the track." His purple and yellow driver's suit confirmed his identity. The Branson boy was clearly upset.

Brent rose from the kart and dropped his helmet on the seat. "You slid off the hairpin by your own doing," he fired back. "I just gave you the room to do it."

Branson lurched angrily. "You clipped me intentionally and my kart has the scuff marks to prove it." He pushed his finger into Brent's chest.

Brent slapped the hand aside. "Those scuff marks were..."

Branson shoved Brent's shoulder. "You're a..."

Brent launched at his rival with both arms extended. Martin jumped in between them, with one arm pushing each boy away from the other. Branson slipped loose from the restraint and reached around to grab at Brent. Brent slapped the hand away again and charged toward him.

Martin grabbed his nephew with both arms while others in the crowd restrained Branson.

"This conversation is over," Martin announced loudly as he attempted to usher Brent away.

"I'm filing a protest!" Branson declared as he was pulled onto pit road. He pointed a finger at Brent. "You're a menace on the race track."

Brent squirmed to look beyond his uncle's hold. "Obviously all that big money of yours can't buy you sportsmanship."

"That's enough, Brent," Martin ordered.

As the congestion opened between them, Brent noticed the other Branson quietly observing from the armor rail. The top of her purple and yellow driver's suit was tied around her waist to reveal a white cotton tank top. The tips of her bob style, coal black hair lay softly against her tanned neck. When her eyes met Brent's stare, she subtly turned away and headed down pit road.

Her despondent brother shook off the arms that constrained him as he looked back at Brent to deliver one last charge. "Bring it on with that antiquated contraption you call a racer."

"I just did," Brent retorted. "And that antiquated contraption just kicked your butt."

"I said that's enough," Martin repeated. "Let it go, Brent."

Katherine Lockeman quietly watched as the crowd dispersed. "Brent, I'm not comfortable with this racing idea of yours."

"I can handle myself, Mom," Brent defended. "That guy is a spoiled jerk. He doesn't scare me."

Martin was more cautious. "Brent, a lot can happen on the race track, and it can be serious. Keep your guard up when dealing with that sort of attitude. The pursuit of victory can often override one's common sense."

From out of the still lingering, small crowd, a red haired girl waved. "Welcome back, Brent." Kimmie Stimpson was an old friend from when Brent raced at Conleyville two years earlier. She lived in a house Uncle Martin built in one of his developments. In fact, it was by her accompanying them to the races that she became better acquainted with a schoolmate, Nate Cormick, a fellow kart racer and aspiring engine mechanic.

Brent was surprised to see her there, and wished she hadn't witnessed the embarrassing encounter. He returned the wave and stepped into his pit space. He was not in the mood for socializing at that moment.

The collection of race officials at the trophy shed confirmed that a protest had indeed been lodged. By the time Martin and Brent arrived to sign for their trophy, the Branson crew had already left.

"Do we have a problem here?" Martin asked the officials calmly.

"A protest was filed against you," the head steward responded. His authority was evidenced by the label on his left shirt pocket. "We had to follow up on it. However, by mutual consensus, the stewards reject the charges made against Mr. Lockeman. The marshal down in Turn 4 saw no intentional aggressiveness on the Lap 8 incident. Being in the position that Mr. Lockeman was in, he could not have pushed the plaintiff off course. In fact, it was reported there was no contact made...at that moment." He then turned his attention to Brent. "I will say though young man, some questionable actions earlier in the race did border on aggressiveness...from both parties involved. We understand some contact in racing may be unavoidable, but I seriously suggest you be more mindful of this conversation going forward. Be warned. We will be watching both of you boys. You are under scrutiny."

CHAPTER 2

KATHERINE LOCKEMAN SAT QUIETLY at the table sipping from her re-warmed cup of coffee when Brent entered the small kitchenette.

While Katherine attended classes to obtain a teaching degree, she had a summer job in a real estate sales office. Luckily for them, Martin and Suz had an apartment Martin recently completed that was a second floor addition to their home. They were welcome to stay there until Katherine got settled since the death of her husband, Brent's father.

"Morning Mom," Brent greeted as he emptied the last of the orange juice from its carton.

Katherine held the coffee cup against her lips with her elbows propped on the table. "I'm concerned about this racing thing you're caught up in," she muttered, staring straight ahead at nothing. "The incident at the track with that angry young man yesterday has me worried."

Brent sat down across from her. "Mom, that was an unusual episode. Unfortunately it happened, but he'll get over it. I have."

She placed her cup on the small round table. "I watched you on the race track, Honey, and I have to be honest, I was scared the entire time. Those kart things you run look dangerously fast. Those races look rough. I saw too much bumping and banging out there." She paused to consider her next statement. "Brent, I lost your father...I can't lose you too." Her eyes were moist from the tears she held back.

Brent lowered his head. "Mom, I lost Dad too. I miss him. But we have to go on living. You know I've always wanted to be a race driver. I have to follow this through...I have to. Uncle Martin and I talked about this. He helped me understand how you feel. But please understand how I feel. Everyone has something inside of them that makes them who they are. I feel like racing is that something for me. Uncle Martin was a state karting champion. He can help me with this."

"Brent, I know you are searching for the missing father figure in your life right now. And Marty is the greatest brother a girl could have. I thank him for being there for you, for us, when we needed him...even now still. But he was finished with racing before you came into his world. He and Suz have their own life and he has a business to run. This racing thing was a fun retreat for him, but he needs to move on. You and I can work this out together."

Brent shook his head. "Mom, we are ready to launch our own kart business. The Avenger Racing kart is almost complete. We plan to introduce it next week at Conleyville." He fixed his eyes on her. "This is what I've wanted for so long. I can't quit now, Mom. I need this for me."

"Honey, Marty has been doing this for you. But

he has to concentrate on his real business now, his building business. This racing stuff is going to end up way too costly and time consuming for him and Suz.

"That didn't come from him, Mom. That's your own opinion."

She shook her head. "Bobby knows a great deal about the housing business and the economic times construction is in right now."

Brent sat back against his chair and raised his arms. "Bobby! So it's Bobby now...not Mr. Wheeling anymore." He looked away in disbelief. "Your boss at the real estate office knows real estate, Mom, real estate...not construction. He's never built a darn thing in his life. He definitely doesn't know the racing business. He knows how to make a sales pitch sound like doctrine. Don't become his next transaction."

Katherine's jaw tightened. "Brent, you talk about what you need. Well, maybe Bobby is what I need right now. I know you don't approve of him. But take the time to get to know him before you pass judgment on the man. He had to know enough about things to get where he is today."

"Real estate, Mom, just real estate...sales actually. Not construction, not racing, not car building. I know more about building a house by working with Uncle Martin than Robert Wheeling knows. And I certainly know more about racing."

Katherine rose from her chair and took her empty cup to the sink. "We'll continue this conversation at a time when you can be more open-minded. As for now, Bobby and I are very good friends...very good friends. I only ask you to respect that."

Brent slid his chair back to get up. "Mom, Mr. Wheeling..."

She turned abruptly to face him. "I said we will continue this some other time. I have to leave for the office. I'll drop you off at Mac's shop."

Mac was the nickname given to Leon McCord, sole proprietor of L&M Hardware, a well stocked hardware and outdoor equipment sales and service center. Mac was one of Martin's old racing buddies from the by-gone days. Martin built the new addition to the rear of his building over a year ago as part of their racing partnership, and to signify Mac's return to karting. In addition to the typical hardware trade, L&M sold and serviced a line of power outdoor equipment. And with their planned expansion into the karting supply market, it was further proposed to be the future home of Avenger Racing.

"Good morning, Mac," Brent welcomed when he was dropped off. He noticed a pair of used lawn mowers in the center of the service area. He enjoyed the experience gained by helping in the shop. "So, what do we have today?"

Mac was at the counter searching part numbers from a thick catalog. "That Bowens there starts up with a shot of ether, but it won't stay running on its own. I'm pulling a new diaphragm from the shelf. Soak the carbs in cleaner and make sure the jets are cleared." He scribbled down a part number. "That's what you get when you leave a gas engine sit with old fuel in it as long as that one has."

Brent frowned. "I just did one of those last week."

"Yeah," Mac recalled, as he laid the new diaphragm on the counter. "Mr. Hoff's." He noticed Brent kneeling beside the second mower. "That one there though…I'm not so sure about. It may be gone…won't run at all. It has spark, but barely any compression. Tear it down and let me know what you find. The owner wants a cheap answer so don't waste a lot of time with it."

"Got it, Boss," Brent chirped as he pulled the Bowens to the work bench. Service work like carburetor rebuilds and blade sharpening had become elementary to him. Following the fundamental rules of small engine repair usually proved sufficient at Brent's level of service work. Mac, on the other hand, a machinist by nature, tackled the more challenging tasks like cutting piston skirts, honing cylinders and polishing valves. While other boys Brent's age could hardly change an oil filter, Brent was sizing piston rings and adjusting centrifugal clutches.

While the Bowens carb soaked in cleaner, Brent pulled the head from the second mower. A hole burnt in the top of the piston, as well as severe scaring of the cylinder wall, confirmed the trouble. The motor was indeed shot.

Mac needed only a peek to concur its demise. "A piece of valve broke off, burnt through the piston and trashed the cylinder. Wow! No wonder the owner said it sounded funny and then just quit. I wonder what fuel he was using." He cupped Brent's shoulder. "Thanks for not spending any more time on it. I'll let him know he needs a whole new mower."

Brent wiped his hands on a shop cloth. "When you said no compression, I went straight to the head to check the valves. What a mess inside there."

He had the Bowens reassembled and three blades sharpened when Mac called him to the back room where he had been quietly working all morning. That was the fabrication area for the new Avenger kart and Mac protected it like it was Fort Knox.

When Brent entered through the doorway, he

stopped in mid-step. There were two racing karts on saw horses. One was a sit-up sprinter similar to what he was currently running. The other was a lay-down enduro similar to what he drove to victory in the Silva 3 Hour Endurance race two years ago.

The enduro, long and narrow in shape, lay open and bare, hardly recognizable as anything for racing. The sprinter, on the other hand, captured Brent's attention. Unlike the usual chassis of welded tubing, it was a steel reinforced composite shell of cross-linked polyethylene and integrated honeycomb, molded in the Midnight Blue color. The body was not the typical smooth fiberglass panels, but instead was a structural tub laced with surface dimples.

Mac stood behind it with a wide grin on his face and his arms outstretched as if to present a priceless, archeological find.

Brent gasped at the prototype, looked up at Mac, and then gaped back at the kart again before stepping farther into the room. A closer examination revealed mounting brackets integrated into the composite configuration.

"Wow!" he muttered. "So this is what you and Uncle Martin meant by the Avenger being a radical variation on a theme. This is far different than anything I even imagined."

Mac waved his hand from the nose of the kart to the tail. "We based our design loosely on the Chaparral race cars of Texan, Jim Hall. Back in the day race cars were aluminum bodies built on heavy steel chassis. The Chaparral was Hall's idea conceived from airplane principles, composite monocoque bodies with movable wings and spoilers. Rather than relying on massive steel framing, Mr. Hall achieved the desired rigidity using extrusion technology. Folks questioned its functionality, but the cars proved themselves quite effective in international competition. They are a part of racing history."

Brent ran his fingers along the side. "So, its strength is in the body itself?"

"Like folds that stiffen up a flat panel…ultra strong yet light weight. The famous Colin Chapman embraced the theory 'add more lightness' to his Lotus race cars."

Brent was excited. "Will it be ready for Conleyville this weekend?"

"Absolutely," Mac assured. "We may have to work late a couple nights, but it'll be ready."

Brent started to leave the room then turned around. "Quantum…they build a good kart don't they?"

Mac nodded. "One of the best Italian karts today. Their shifter karts are dominating the competition in Europe and South America. They just recently hit the U.S. market. You met a pair of Quantums. They're doing quite well. A lot of outfits have their eye on them."

"The Branson crew is running them," Brent said. "I had a little run-in with the Branson boy at Conleyville."

Mac supported his arms on the Avenger. "Marty mentioned it. Harrison Branson is a hot head. I've heard about him. You stole his thunder and that's how he reacts. Watch him. He's long on talent but short on temper. You're not the first one to get in his way."

Brent processed the information. "What's up with the sister? I mean, how is she with all of this?"

"Harris and Hannah are twins, if you can believe twins can be so polar. She has the patience, charm and sweetness that didn't make it into his gene pool. He's arrogant, she's shy. Other than that, I can't tell you much more about them."

"I want to beat Branson and his Quantum," Brent blurted. "I want the Avenger to bring him down a notch."

Mac's grin vanished. "Brent, our marketing plan is really, really simple. We promote our product positively and professionally, no animosity. Don't get hung up on the little things. Remember that tiny piece of valve in the lawn mower engine? It fused itself to the piston and burned a hole through it. That little thing wasted the whole motor." He paused to let his words sink in. "Don't be like that piece of valve. Let Branson go."

CHAPTER 3

JUST AS MAC HAD SUGGESTED, WORK on the two Avengers spilled over into the evening hours. The usual customer business during regular hours barred any work on the karts. But with Martin's assistance in the evenings, the project moved along.

Mac fabricated jigs to replicate the steel reinforcing in each kart to use on additional bodies. Steel parts in future models would be sent out to be powder-coated, but in an effort to save time on the prototypes, the present pieces were primed and painted.

An adjustable dual cylinder braking system supplied stopping power to all four wheels, and wet cassette bearings provided a zero drag axle rotation. Unlike the side mounted fuel tanks common in the typical enduro kart, Mac's own designed chambered tank was located just forward of the steering wheel upright, nestled between the driver's legs. He thought that location would eliminate sloshing and the possibility of fuel starvation under heavy cornering.

Using Brent as a model, Martin helped to mount

the seats and steering components, all of which were adjustable for different drivers.

By midweek Brent was clear-coating the sprint body's blue finish. At that point in his racing experience, every step of the assembly process was routine. He understood it all except for the tiny dimples in the body, which he wondered about all week.

"I always thought aerodynamics meant smooth bodywork for efficient air flow," he mentioned during a break one evening.

Mac nodded. "With a bullet style frontal area, yes, that is the case. But we have to move air around a broader mass. The Chaparral cars were an experiment in aerodynamics." He went to a drawer in his workbench and returned with a golf ball. "What is it that makes this ball travel so fast and far through the air?"

"It is round?" Brent guessed.

Mac shook his head. "It's the dimples. The ball actually rides on all of these tiny pockets of air."

Brent considered the theory. "So, that will work the same way on our kart?"

"At sprint tracks like Conleyville, perhaps not so much. But on an enduro course with those long straightaways and the speeds they have…that's like this golf ball soaring over a fairway."

Brent saw very little of his mother during the week, which guiltily he considered was probably a blessing in disguise. She dropped him off at the shop every day, but they didn't talk. He preferred not having to discuss Robert Wheeling with her. Since she was seeing more and more of the man, he knew there would be no avoiding the subject if they were together in the same room for any length of time. Uncle Martin took him back home each night when they finished at the shop.

Arrangements were made to use the Conleyville track on Saturday as a test and tune day. For a nominal fee, the track was rented for the private session, thereby avoiding unwanted exposure.

The sit-up sprint was the most logical choice for the test. The lay-down model would never test well on a tight sprint track even with facility correct gearing. Besides, there was still extensive work required on the enduro unit.

Although starting out mild and partly cloudy, the forecast for Saturday promised a hot and sunny transition by noon. The gloomy weather accentuated the desolate atmosphere when they arrived. Brent had never seen the facility when it wasn't bustling with activity. The emptiness seemed almost eerie. Yet, somehow, it felt like the perfect setting for the Avenger's trial run.

The kart's Midnight Blue color glistened even in the partial sunshine of morning. Its lines flashed like bolts of lightning from the clear-coat finish. The front spoiler framed the fresh new tires and chrome wheels giving it a secure, sure-footed appearance.

To spare the brand new engine Mac had just blueprinted, he installed a used one on the kart for the day. The purpose for the testing was to dial in the chassis, not tune an engine.

Unloaded and raring to go, Brent stood motionless beside the kart. "If appearance imitates performance, this thing is gonna be fast."

Mac relayed some preliminary instructions as Brent fastened the strap of his helmet and pulled his driving gloves on. "Let me warn you right up front...you will experience over-steer. We purposely designed the kart to scoot around these tight sprint corners. I can make steering adjustments for the longer endurance tracks. Just be aware of it so you don't get in over your head. So, take a few laps to get comfortable and signal me when you're ready to open it up."

Brent closed his face shield and nodded. Then Martin added, "You already know the racing groove here. Use the entire track…in wide, squeeze the apex, out wide. Be as smooth and consistent as you can. We want to monitor how well the kart tracks."

Brent gave a thumbs up. "Got it!" He settled into the seat. Starter engaged. Vroom! The Avenger burst onto the straightaway.

Heading toward Turn 1 he jerked the steering wheel from side to side and tapped the brake pedal to test the kart's reflexes. He glided effortlessly through the corner, still accelerating, and set up to sweep Turn 2. Drifting wide, he committed himself for the first serious cornering test at Turn 3. Riding the outside edge of pavement he stabbed the brake pedal and threw the wheel to the left.

The Avenger squealed and then swung frantically across the track. Heading for the downgrade, it broke traction and started to spin.

With his heart pounding, he wrenched the wheel to the right, trying to stay on course. Sliding through the middle of the turn and back to the outside, his right tires hooked off the edge and tossed him onto the grass, out of control.

His hands wrestled the steering wheel as his foot punched the brake. No traction on the grass. All four tires had locked up while clawing for precious grip. He slid across Turn 4 sideways and shot onto the grass off the other side.

He steered to the right, determined to get pointed back in the right direction. Volleying delicately between brake and throttle, he felt the rear tires finally bite. The kart straightened and aimed itself toward the top of the hill.

Once again under control, he crested the hill, swept the esses and floated through Turn 10, barely nicking the apex. As he unwound onto the front straight, he saw Uncle Martin waving for him to stop. He lifted from the accelerator and coasted to a stop on the start-finish line.

Mac and Martin both looked solemn.

"What was that all about at the hairpin?" Martin asked curtly.

Brent flipped open his face shield. "It was more aggressive than I expected."

Mac knelt down beside him. "I told you to go easy until you're comfortable. You're not used to the over-steer. You were to do a couple of laps first and not get in over your head, remember?" He quickly surveyed the kart. "Is everything alright otherwise?"

"Yes," Brent humbly nodded. "I'm sorry. I just pushed the kart too soon."

Martin exhaled a calming breath. "No, Brent, you pushed yourself too soon. Now, learn from that. Always know where you are out there…with the kart and with your head. You didn't know where you were. Get control from the top down, not the bottom up."

Brent hung his head and nodded. "I got it this time. Can we try it again?"

Mac stood up. "I'll be looking for your signal…when you're ready this time."

Restart. Easing away from the line, Brent let the kart feel its way. Drifting wide out of Turn 1, he made a long arc to include Turn 2 in the same maneuver. Then he eased it through Turn 3 and down the hill. He braked gently and observed the bite. Smooth hairpin. The Avenger felt confident entering the corners and sure-footed coming out. Up the incline and steady through the esses the kart purred like a kitten.

Brent felt ready, settled and eager. The kart felt ready and willing. Passing the starting line he signaled. It was throttle down.

The Avenger blasted into Turn 1 drifting wide. Apex and then to the outside, it brushed through Turn 2. With the clearing of clouds, the sun highlighted a radiant blue streak down the backstretch. The whine of a full throttled 2-cycle engine resonated off the pavement.

The Avenger dove into Turn 3 with only a chirp of protest from sweltering rubber. At the bottom of the hill the tires smoked under hard braking as they grabbed for traction. Any remnants of an earlier off-road excursion were nonexistent.

Though reluctant at first, Brent began to realize the over-steer designed into the steering geometry required less effort on his part to negotiate the turns. The less he forced it, the better the kart performed. It did indeed scoot around the corners, just as Mac had explained.

Lap after lap the Avenger rode the course with consistency, like a slot car on a toy track. Brent became more acclimated with each circuit. Martin finally waved him in after twelve laps.

"That looked much better," Martin commended. "How did it feel once you let the kart do its job?"

Brent removed his helmet and ruffled a hand through his hair. "It practically drove itself once I stopped fighting it. The over-steer is great when you get used to it. It was scary at first though."

Mac read the tire wear and noted some scuffing on

the inside of the front tires. "We need less camber to get the contact patch squared up. That will soften the over-steer too. I plan to offer spindles in a few optional degrees. But overall, the kart appeared to stick well."

Brent rose from the driver seat to stretch. "Let's just go with the correct spindle geometry we need and forget about options."

"Camber should be adjustable from track to track, or from one driver to another," Mac explained. "With a few available options, it's simply a matter of popping out the king pins and swapping out the spindle. That would allow chassis tuning to a drivers' preference. Some people like more camber, some less. And besides, it's a great marketing option."

Brent frowned. "I keep forgetting it's not just about us anymore."

"That's right," Martin replied. "When we beat the competition with our own design, we invite them, hopefully encourage them, to buy our product. It's the way of corporate America. It's survival. If you want something better, you do something different. Otherwise what you have is only as good as any other product."

Mac agreed. "Well put, Marty."

Brent opened the top of his driver suit and absorbed the serenity of the track, the stark contrast of what it will be like when the gates open the next day. "Are we ready guys?"

Martin grinned. "I'd say so." He fumbled with the stop watch that hung from his neck. "Your times matched your regular ETs for here, and that was with a used motor. Tomorrow should be interesting."

"And our new motor is ready to go, Mac?" Brent asked.

"It was broke in on the bench with special lube. I

compared the port castings on three different cylinder jugs and used the best of the three. It dyno'd great. So, yeah," Mac grinned. "I'd say it's ready."

CHAPTER 4

KATHERINE WAS PUTTING DISHES from the sink into the cupboard when Brent returned home. By then it was early evening since he and Martin stayed at the shop to swap out the engine on the kart for the race the next day.

"So how did your race go today?" she asked. It was the first real sentence she spoke to him all week. She seemed overly cheery.

"We race tomorrow," Brent replied. "Today was a test day to break the Avenger in. But it went okay, better than I expected."

"That's good," she said as she reached to a higher shelf with some plates.

"Let me help you, Mom," Brent offered as he took the plates from her. "We're hoping for a grand performance tomorrow." He looked at her closely. "You look spiffy this evening. What's up?"

"Spiffy!" she exclaimed. "Wow, then maybe I should change into something more appropriate. I'm not sure I want spiffy."

"Okay," Brent countered, turning to face her. "You're all dressed up. What gives?"

"Can't a woman dress a little special if she feels like it?"

"Come on, Mom, give," Brent insisted. "That's not like you. What's going on?"

She smiled playfully. "I thought you'd be out late again and Bobby invited me out for the evening. He'll be here shortly," she beamed.

Brent closed his eyes. It was the very topic he wanted to avoid. "Mom, I thought we…"

The smile left her face. "Brent, the man asked me out to dinner. I accepted. That is my decision to make."

"You're getting too serious with him, Mom."

"It's dinner Brent, nothing more. I feel like I can use an evening out for once. Surely I have the right." Her mouth quivered as she managed to control a rush of emotion. "I hoped you would understand. I hoped at least you could wish me a nice evening."

Brent supported his arms on the countertop behind him. "I worry about you, that's all."

"I worry about you too but it doesn't seem to persuade you to stop racing."

"Mom, that's not even the same," Brent declared. "We don't know Mr. Wheeling's intentions."

"Intentions," she mused. "Honey, it is dinner…in a public restaurant. I'm thankful for your concern, Brent, truly I am. And if anything more should come of it, you and I will definitely have a heart-to-heart. But as for now, I'm a big enough girl to decide to go out to dinner with a man. I feel like a nice dinner with a nice man at a nice place. Can't you please support me just once?"

Brent hung his head. "You're right. It is your decision. You deserve a nice time out for once." He hesitated with his next thought. "Mom, I just don't trust him." There, he finally said it. It was out in the open.

Katherine approached him with her arms out-stretched. "I can see that, though I don't know why you would feel that way. You don't even know him."

"He's a jerk!"

She pulled away. "That's enough! I don't want to hear that again."

Just then an SUV pulled into the driveway. A vehicle door closed, followed by the clickity-clack of hard soled shoes on the brick pavers that led to the second floor entrance. The doorbell rang.

Katherine adjusted the tail of her blouse and flattened her skirt. "Come in Bobby!" Then she kissed Brent on the cheek. "Warm up some lasagna from the fridge for yourself later. What are your plans for the night now?"

Robert Wheeling stepped into the room from the stairway. Even in casual attire he was a sharp dresser, well groomed, with a spa obtained tan and picture perfect hair.

"Well hello there, Brent, my boy," he smiled instantaneously as if greeting a new prospect at the front door of a real estate showing. "How is the race car business going?"

"We hope to find out real soon," Brent replied. He looked at his mother to address her still open question. "We're leaving for the track early. I'm tired. I'll probably just sack out." He grinned at her. "It's not like I have a driver's license and can go off somewhere."

She gave a curt wave of her hand. "That will come all too soon."

The smile was still on Mr. Wheeling's face, as if it was a permanent fixture. "Ah yes, the proverbial license to drive. I remember it well."

Katherine read Brent's yearning to respond, but shut it down with a drilling glare.

*****

The Conleyville gates had been open for a half hour by the time the Avenger party arrived. Aunt Suz accompanied Martin, Mac and Brent for the novelty of unveiling their new marque. They rolled it from the trailer to the wonder of those present. It created a whirlwind of curiosity. What was this unorthodox kart and where was it from?

Kimmie Stimpson was in the next pit helping her friend Nate set up a table to display his customer's motors for pickup. "Brent!" she yelled. "What are you boys up to now?" She grabbed Nate by the arm to accompany her for a closer look.

Brent grinned and continued to unload the trailer. Kimmie was still the same bubbly girl he remembered her to be. And her hair was still as fire red as ever.

Folks began to gather around, nobody talking, everyone just looking. Nate stepped closer for a more detailed look. "Humm, full composite body...interesting. It's catching on in the big boy ranks. I wondered when it would show up in karting. What kind of performance numbers do you have on it?"

Brent shook his friend's hand. "Don't really have any yet. We just did the maiden run yesterday. It is literally just off the drawing board."

"I wish you luck with it," Nate said. "I admire innovation. You know I'm a tinkerer myself. I like thinking outside the box."

The pits continued to fill up as more race teams arrived. Even before tech officially opened, spectators were filing into the bleachers.

Martin excused himself through a group of onlookers to get to Brent. "Let's get up to tech for inspection. I have the push stick."

The crowd opened as Brent hooked the push stick to the steering wheel and guided the Avenger onto pit road. The new model commanded attention. Even the Branson crew took notice as Brent rolled past the Quantum pit. Harris studied Brent's kart. Hannah studied Brent. Now knowing they were indeed twins, Brent realized they really did look alike, right down to their stallion black hair. Harrison's was long for a boy while Hannah's could be considered cropped for a girl. But outwardly, there was no denying they were brother and sister.

The senior tech inspector taunted Martin when he saw the Avenger. "What did you bring me today, Kessick, more aggravation like the old days?"

Martin grabbed his greeting hand and pretended to twist it off his arm. "You're still sticking karts, ay, Frank? When are you ever gonna just bite the bullet and actually race one?"

The inspector laughed. "I'm too busy trying to keep you old chumps on the track." He shook his head as he surveyed the Avenger. "So, Marty, are you modeling Chaparral now or what?"

"Just scratching an itch with some experimental concepts. Racing has been the automotive think tank ever since Ray Harroun won the Indy 500 back in 1911. He shocked everyone when he stuck a rearview mirror in his Marmon Wasp so he wouldn't have to haul his mechanic around the whole race. It changed auto racing forever."

Frank pumped the brake pedal with his hand and discovered a missing safety pin. "Yeah, Marty, but we still have to have cotter pins or double nuts on brakes and steering. Safety things will never change."

Martin shrugged. "Hey, I have to leave something for you to find so you can keep us old chumps on the track."

If anyone present was not aware of the Avenger by then, they were when the track opened for practice. The track announcer, always searching for fill-in material, challenged everyone to watch for the blue, all new Avenger Racing's debut in the Yamaha sprint class.

Knowing all eyes would be on him, Brent went on the track for his first practice session with apprehension. Mac tried to ease his anxiety. "Show, but don't blow. Mix it up enough to whet their appetite, and then bring it in before the session is over. Save it for qualifying."

Both Quantums entered the track right behind Brent, made two laps and then pitted. Brent pitted as planned two laps later.

To protect it from the chaos up front, Martin purposely registered the Avenger late so it would start the qualifying race in the last row. It was no surprise on the grid that the front row was all purple and yellow. The Bransons were persistently at the top of their game.

At the drop of the green flag, Brent immediately advanced two rows, from twelfth to eighth, with his habitual dash to the outside. By the hairpin he was in seventh and by the esses he had taken over the sixth spot.

The PA system spewed the name Avenger in practically every sentence, twice the promotion the name Quantum received. At the checkered flag the Quantums nailed down the top two positions. Brent was fifth.

Kimmie was waiting in the pit with Aunt Suz to greet him after the cool down lap. "First showing, awesome! Brent, you never leave me disappointed."

Brent was still in the seat when Mac examined the wear on the front tires. "I have to make up those replacement spindles soon. I can tell already there's too much scuffing on the inside. We'll run new rubber for the race."

Martin helped Brent up and guided him alongside the trailer out of earshot. "The Bransons had a full second and a half on you. Is anything wrong?"

"The clutch bogs on engagement, especially up the hill coming out of Four," Brent answered. "But then you did want me to sandbag it a little."

Martin gripped his shoulder. "Just making sure. I'll slip the clutch a few hundred revs for the race."

Brent decided against his usual stroll down pit road after qualifying. Except for perhaps with Kimmie and Nate, he had no desire to socialize. He surely would not talk racing with the Bransons. Nor would he indulge the inquisitive minds of those who would bombard him about the Avenger. And all the other racers were consumed with their own rituals.

So he sat on a stack of tires beside Aunt Suz as she calmly read a book. But he was fidgety. He eventually chose to shed his driver suit and watch some action from the pit bleachers incognito.

When he finally returned to his pit he realized how much he needed that time to disconnect. At some point while engaging the inquiring onlookers, Mac and Martin managed to have the tires, clutch and fuel ready to go for him. The only thing Brent had to prepare was his mind.

At the call for Yamaha Sprint, Brent suited up and followed Martin and the Avenger through the crowd to the pre-grid.

Martin parked it on the inside of the third row. "You're okay, right?" he asked.

"Yeah," Brent answered. "Thanks for taking care of everything. I needed some down time."

"We knew that. Suz said you were restless. So we let you have your time alone."

Brent watched the grid fill up. It was a repeat of the previous week. He was starting in fifth place again and the well funded Quantums had again seized the front spots. Last week he felt he was the underdog to their high dollar advantage. He hoped that was all about to change.

He fastened his helmet. "Hello again twins," he mumbled to himself.

Even the pace lap duplicated the previous week. The Bransons set a pace to purposely restrict the rest of the field. Then again, just as before, they blasted away from Turn 10 leaving everyone behind, including Brent. But unlike the previous week, he was trapped along the rail. His competitors did not anticipate the Branson strategy like he did, and he was not in any position to prevent it.

The pack was tight all the way to the backstretch where a gap finally opened in the row ahead. Impatient for the opportunity, Brent dove between the two karts and held his line under heavy braking for Turn 3. Down the hill he edged ahead of the pair and got a better setup for the hairpin at the bottom. He was clear of them by the esses.

The Bransons were halfway to the start-finish line when Brent lunged out of Turn 10. "You're not getting away from me now folks," he muttered.

By Turn 1 he erased half of that lead. The Quantums sped smoothly through Turn 2 side-by-side but Harris out braked his sister in Turn 3 to jump ahead. Hannah quickly choked up behind him.

Brent had them reeled in by the bottom of the hill.

Hannah tucked in tight to her brother along the inside. Brent danced tenderly between throttle and brake and drifted wide. The Avenger clung on to the outside edge, pulled alongside Hannah on the climb up the hill and inched up beside Harris through the esses.

By holding his position, Brent had stolen the inside for Turn 10. Harris was not one to forfeit. He attempted to muscle his way over but Brent would not surrender either.

Bang!

They went through the bend like Siamese twins joined at the hip with Hannah glued to their tails. Brent saw the Quantum beside him wiggle but it stayed planted and crouched. Neither contender lifted from the accelerator.

Commanding the inside groove, Brent swept onto the main straight, edging ahead of Harris. He felt a nudge from behind as Hannah took up the draft, apparently choosing him as the better option over her brother. By the starting line their draft powered them fully clear of Harris. Now leading the race and having a clear track ahead, Brent kicked the throttle to the floor to maintain his position.

Hannah would not wane from behind. She pressed him all the way into Turn 1. On the short chute that fed into the sweeper, the Avenger broke free and picked up half a length. It became a full length by the back straight. The pair of Quantums reunited in his wake and chased him down with a new draft of their own.

Turn 3, the downhill jaunt and the hairpin at the bottom provided an even greater gap for Brent. The Avenger was doing its job. It rode the groove like it was on rails.

Anxious to regain the coveted lead, Harris

frantically slung his mount through the slithering esses while Hannah held hers smooth and defined. It paid her dividends. She came out of Turn 10 pulling away from him. Her brother's manic ambition was costing him valuable yardage.

Passing the starting line, Brent saw Martin and Mac waving him on from behind pit wall. It was a standing audience in the bleachers. The Avenger was building a credible first impression and the track announcer made it public. Brent went unchallenged for three laps and piloted his way into a half-lap lead.

On Lap 8 he chased the first two stragglers downhill toward the hairpin. It was brake, apex and throttle. Then he soared up the hill and passed them both in the same motion.

Suddenly the rhythmic chorus of his exhaust died without warning. His freshly built new motor shut down with a single 'dah'. With no power, the Avenger slumbered through the esses only to coast to a disappointing halt in the grass.

The baffled glares of the two Bransons as they passed did little to relieve the sick feeling Brent had in his stomach.

CHAPTER 5

AFTER THE CHECKERED FLAG FLEW once again for the Quantum duo, the rescue squad went on the track to pick up the non-finishers. Exactly which Branson took home the victory flag was of no interest to Brent. He only knew it wasn't going home with him. What he hoped would be a glorious first outing for Avenger Racing wound up being a depressing DNF, a big fat Did Not Finish.

"Chalk another one up for the competition," he grumbled.

When the tow rope dropped him at his pit, Brent faced the stares of his crew and at least a dozen curious onlookers.

Mac seemed to be the most discouraged of the entire crowd. "What in blazes happened out there?" he fumed. "You were killing the competition."

Brent got out of the kart and dropped his helmet, neck brace and gloves on the seat. "Stuck!"

"That was a brand new motor," Mac argued. "I broke it in on the bench myself."

"Easy, Mac," Martin injected calmly. "I doubt it was anything Brent did. Let's get it back to the shop, pull the head and see what it looks like inside."

No one else in the crowd said a word. Everyone watched as Martin pushed the Avenger off pit road to the trailer. Mac returned from the tool chest armed with a ratchet and socket. "I need to see this right now for myself."

Martin was uncomfortable with the audience gathering around them. "We're done here today, Mac. There's nothing we can do here right now to change anything. Let's get it back to the shop and open it up there."

Kimmie and Nate slipped through the mob to join Brent by the Avenger. "Brent, you were cleaning up out there," Kimmie remarked. "What happened?"

Nate stared down at the engine and answered her question. "I heard it go pulling the hill. He stuck a ring."

Brent wiped his forehead then tossed the rag aside. "It just went dead…no bang…no clang…just a dah."

Nate concurred. "Yeah, that's what I mean. The piston seized in the cylinder and went…dah. Those two-stroke Yamahas do that."

Avenger Racing was finished for the day. They loaded their equipment and left the track before the program of races even began. The ride home was quiet. There wasn't much to discuss. The Avenger had outclassed the competition. It out ran, out braked and out cornered anything on the race track. But to win, it had to finish. And it didn't.

The whole way home Brent chewed on the thought that defeat had been yanked right from the jaws of victory. Failure had a sour taste. Regardless of how sound a concept may be or how innovative a design is, with a weak link in the performance chain, the chain snaps.

Upon returning to the shop, Mac could not resist the gnawing urge to pull the Yamaha head and cylinder. Brent helped him hoist it onto the stand and watched the tear-down commence. As Mac lifted the jug from the block halves, metallic shavings sprinkled from the cylinder bore. Deep scratches on the piston skirt concluded a snapped wrist pin clip to be the culprit. Scarring on the cylinder wall acknowledged the same.

Mac shook his head with pressed lips. "A circlip! Can you believe it? A wrist pin circlip snapped and lodged between the piston and cylinder. The friction seized the motor." He dropped his head. "Beaten by a two bit clip!"

Brent shrugged. It was time to accept fate and move on. "Can we be ready for the Somerton Enduro next week?"

Martin slapped the rear tire with enthusiasm. "Mac, you have to finish the lay-down for next week. I'll do a full top-end rebuild on this motor. This jug is too far gone to hone. Brent, can you carry Mac's customer load this week?"

"Sure. And what can I do for Avenger Racing?"

"That's what you can do for Avenger Racing," Martin replied. "We all have to pick up the loose ends. Somerton Motor Park is our first contest on the national circuit. We have to look at this seriously."

Mac agreed. "A sponsorship deal would be nice about now too. This is where the nickel has to become dollars."

The week that followed was a busy one. Martin was wrapping up a commercial construction project during the day and building a new racing motor at night.

Mac appropriated whatever time he could spare from the hardware business to finish the Avenger enduro. By design, it was more strategic than the sprinter; longer, narrower and lower.

While Mac fabricated the spare spindles they needed from stock material, Brent could see their material supply was depleting. "Are you going to reorder material?" he asked.

"I have a list ready," Mac answered. "I just have to get a check sent out to cover it."

Brent thought no more about it at the time. His week was consumed with the rudimentary tasks of blade sharpening, carburetor cleaning and such. He wanted to be hands on with the further development of the Avenger, but he resigned himself to his assigned duty, which was keeping Mac freed up. While doing so he uncovered a quandary; why did their work load always seem to increase in proportion with the racing obligation? When time was most valuable, they seemed to have less of it.

On Wednesday evening, Katherine left a message at the shop that she had to stay for a meeting after work. When she finally did step in the door at 9:30, Brent had just finished eating a bowl of soup he made.

"I kept a bowl on the stove for you," Brent told his mother.

She placed a bundle of papers on the table. "Thank you, Honey, but I already ate."

"You ate at your after work meeting?"

"No. Bobby took me to a nice restaurant."

Brent turned to put his empty bowl in the sink. "So your meeting was with Bobby, not the office?"

She shuffled the bundle of papers. "So I had dinner with Bobby."

Brent pivoted around. "Why did you lead

everyone to believe you had a real estate meeting?"

She turned to face her son straight on. "I told Marty I had a meeting after work. That's what I told him because that's what I had...a meeting after work. I find it insulting to think I have to fill in all the minute details of my activities to everyone."

"It was a date with that Wheeling jerk, Mom. Call it what it was."

"It was a meeting," she snapped. "It was a meeting to discuss something with a dear friend. So what if it included dinner?"

"I don't want you seeing him!"

"That is not your decision to make, Brent!"

"I'm not comfortable with him, Mom."

"And I'm not comfortable with your motor racing, Son, but are you going to stop?"

The kitchen was uncannily silent. Brent opened the dishwasher door and began loading it with dishes from the sink. Katherine gathered her papers from the table and moved them to the opposite counter.

Several minutes passed, a thick several minutes. Then Brent stepped toward the hallway to leave. "Goodnight, Mom."

Katherine met him in the archway and hugged him. "Brent, Honey, we can work all this out. I just ask that you stand with me in this. We only have each other right now. Cherish today because we don't yet have tomorrow."

Brent hugged his mother closely. "Why must you bring Mr. Wheeling into the picture? We're doing just fine without him around."

"That depends on your interpretation of fine," she sniffled. "Fine has a different meaning to different people."

Brent exhaled. "Wow, Mom. That's getting way too deep now. I guess I really don't want to get into all that after all. Goodnight."

CHAPTER 6

THE NATIONAL ENDURANCE CIRCUIT has a taste and feel of the major league of auto racing. Endurance races are run on specially built, closed road courses around the country, tracks that are home to sanctioned sports car, motorcycle and karting events. Brent's one and only exposure to such a long course event was the Silva 3 Hour Endurance race at Randoff Field two years ago. It left an indelible mark on him. As he gained more racing experience, he knew such venues would become his stomping ground. He would transition from local small sprint tracks to the bigger, longer courses.

In addition to the local and regional drawing card, national races bring top programs and prestige to an area. Locals get a chance to defend their turf against their invading, traveling rivals. It separates the doers from the wannabees.

Somerton Motor Park was a two hour drive northwest for the Avenger team. It was a 2½ mile, 13 turn road course that twisted and meandered through a once prosperous stone quarry.

The paddock area was still relatively empty when the Avenger trailer rolled through the gate. But those who were present took notice when the ramp door dropped and the two Midnight Blue composite racers emerged into the sunlight. Although no one commented, it was no secret by the looking and pointing, their curiosity was aroused.

Nate and Kimmie arrived shortly thereafter and set up in the neighboring pit. While Nate set out his line of parts and accessories for sale, Kimmie found pleasure from laying in the new Avenger Enduro and having her picture taken. Brent even commented how her long, distinctive red hair contrasted nicely with the Avenger's striking blue color.

By the time safety tech opened, Brent had both karts fueled and practice tires installed. Other than some rules interpretation with the tech man concerning bodywork, there were no safety or technical issues. Both Avengers received track clearance stickers.

The agenda progressed quickly. Following a brief drivers meeting under the scoring tower, the track opened for sprint practice. But pit lane was jam-packed with all kart classes...sprint, enduro and shifters, anxious to go out with their respective groups. New motors would be broken in, clutch settings checked and gear ratios tested. For some newcomers to the track like Brent and Martin, it would be the only chance to learn the course before the actual race; to figure out turn-in and brake points, exit lines and surface grip.

Nate and Brent left pit lane together. Since Nate had driven the unusual counter-clockwise direction of Somerton Park before, he led.

Turn 1 was a sharp and flat, decreasing radius turn, but faster than it appeared to be. If not for the Turn

2 chicane to avoid a pond, it would be a fast shoot into the long radius of Turn 3. Then came a tunnel, Turn 4, and the incline to the higher elevated next four turns. After crossing back over the tunnel, the half mile long back straight ran along the ridge behind the paddock. An acute Turn 9 began the descent into the hairpin and the succeeding Turn 11, the first half of the esses. For a quarry course, the esses offered ample run-off room. Turn 13 was a classic left hander that dumped onto the ¾ mile main straightaway.

The Avenger tracked smooth and effortless. Brent made mental notes of peculiar conditions around the course to help him adapt. Ten laps later the checkered flag ended the session. Tow trucks rescued the breakdowns and the track prepared for the first enduro round of practice.

Brent whipped the kart in alongside Martin who was ready to go out with the lay-down. "It's a pretty easy course, I think," he reported. "We may want to add one gear tooth because of the hill. See what you think."

Martin fastened his helmet strap. "Anything else?"

"The track has good grip, especially going into the hairpin, more than you would expect."

"Good. Thank you. I'll see you in a bit." They exchanged high fives.

An explosive wail of exhausts accompanied the horde of enduros that blasted onto the track. Martin pulled out in the midst of them.

Brent looked up and down pit road for a sign of his two purple and yellow adversaries. There was none. Perhaps the Bransons chose to avoid the frantic practice. Surely they wouldn't avoid the weekend entirely. There were substantial championship points at stake.

He joined Mac along pit wall to wait for Martin to come around. "I don't see the 'Go-Lightning' bunch," he said after Martin passed. "You don't suppose they skipped do you?"

Mac supported himself on his elbows on the wall. "Not a chance. They're here. I saw their trailer pull in while you were on the track. They'll probably wait until near the end to go out to conceal their hand as long as possible."

Brent frowned. "That would be a good strategy for us if we didn't need the track time to learn the course."

Nate was discussing engine instructions with a customer so Kimmie joined Brent along pit wall.

After watching the practice for a couple laps, impatience set in. "Do you want to walk around the paddock with me?" Brent asked her.

"Sure, why not." she beamed. "Maybe we'll discover some ancient relic left over from the old quarry pits." After a moment of silence, she giggled. "You want to check on her don't you?"

Brent huffed. "Check on who? What are you talking about?"

She took on a slanted smile. "You know who. We all noticed your eye for her...that tall slender thing. Brent, I know you. You may have just moved back into my town after being away for two years, but you haven't changed all that much. And just in case you haven't noticed what everyone else has...she has an eye for you too."

A wave of smugness washed through his veins, a wave he dared not let show. "Hannah Branson is just a strong competitor to watch out for."

"See," Kimmie teased. "You do know who I'm

talking about. Just be careful you don't get them confused. Her brother Harrison is the one you need to watch out for, not Hannah. Don't cross his path. He has a very strong willpower."

"So do I," Brent countered firmly. "Besides, I already crossed his path."

"I know, I was there," she chuckled. "Come on, follow me. I'll take you to your eye candy."

The paddock had filled up with racing teams, trailers and karts of all sizes and colors. One odd prospect that caught Brent's eye was a crude looking sprint kart sitting on a wooden crate outside a tent. Its bodywork was duct taped together like a patched quilt. He remembered seeing it on the race track during practice and recalled thinking how out of sorts it appeared, especially on the National circuit.

Kimmie saw him eye it up as they passed. "That's the Colton boys. Nate says their stuff is all used equipment, never anything new, and they're usually pretty fast. In fact, they lead the series right now in driver points. But they're really private...you never see them out and about. They're from out of the mountainous region somewhere. A strange pair."

As they wandered further along through the lively paddock, Brent spotted the purple and yellow Branson karts along the back fence. Harris was busy mixing a jug of racing fuel while Hannah checked tire pressures on her kart. The top of her driver's suit was rolled down and tied around her waist. Though still a distance down pit road, when she looked up, she spotted Brent and Kimmie walking. That's when Brent turned around to leave.

"Chicken!" Kimmie teased as she turned around with him.

"Hey, you're the one who said we were checking

out these old quarry pits for some ancient relic."

"Sure, like you bought into that play-on-words," she snickered. "Chicken!"

When they returned to their pit, Martin was back from practice, surrounded by a group of racers examining the pair of Avengers. He was answering their questions but he was discrete with his answers. After all, even though the exposure was fine, there was only so much he wanted to reveal.

Brent went back out on the track when it opened for sprinters again. He ran solo and took it smooth, no flashiness. He just read the course and occasionally stabbed the throttle to evaluate grip and gearing. Although the Avenger felt good, he concluded it did need a tooth added to the gear ratio. He was careful not to let anyone size him up.

When he returned to the pit, he got his first opportunity to confer with Martin about the practice sessions.

"You were right about the gearing," Martin said. "One more tooth for the hill should put us in the range we want. Good call. It was an easy track to read. I don't need another round." Being a former champion, Martin had a method for reading a new track.

"I want to make my gear change and go out at least one more time," Brent said. "I hope to be ready then too."

He changed the rear sprocket and broke for lunch. He was one of the first to be on pit lane for the start of afternoon practice. Again, it was a packed field. Everyone still seemed to be sorting out their equipment, trying to tweak their final set-up. And again, there was no sign of the Bransons.

He tried to avoid the frenzy. He didn't want to get

caught up in the mayhem of the crowd. But each time he backed off to escape one pack, he dropped back into the ranks of another. It was much too busy. Frustrated, he returned to the pits before the session ended.

"I'm done now too." Brent reported. "It's not worth the risk out there. I'm ready to race tomorrow."

"Sounds good," Martin agreed. "Let's spare our equipment and pack it up for the day."

When the next sprint practice was announced, the trailer was almost loaded. Brent noticed the two Quantums pushing their way to the grid. As they passed by, Harris peeked for a glimpse of the Avenger but quickly looked away. Brent thought he detected a slight smile on Hannah's face.

He turned to Martin. "I think I'd like to watch this practice."

"Go ahead," Martin said. "We'll head out when you get back."

Kimmie walked along with him to the pit wall. "Brent, I know you don't like hearing this, but you should lay low with regards to Hannah Branson. I'm being serious now. I've been on this circuit these two years you've been away. She's rich, she's smart and she's tough."

"Three things about a girl scare a guy," Brent bantered "That she's rich, she's smart and she's pretty."

Kimmie laughed. "That's funny…I didn't say pretty. Is that what scared you about me when we first met?"

Brent fought back a grin. "Gee, I didn't know you were rich."

Kimmie searched his face for a sign of jest. "Good save there Lockeman, good save. I'll assume you had a compliment hidden in there somewhere."

CHAPTER 7

TRAVELING ON THE NATIONAL CIRCUIT typically requires lodging or camping at the track where permitted. But since they cut out early and Somerton Motor Park was only a two hour drive, Martin decided to return home for the night. They left their equipment locked in the trailer at their pit.

Katherine and Bobby Wheeling were both in the living room when Brent arrived. Naturally Katherine was surprised to see him home. "I thought you guys were going to be off racing all weekend," she confessed.

Brent avoided eye contact. "Yeah, I see that."

Katherine's face hardened as she pondered the inference. "Brent..."

Bobby stood up and interjected. "Hey there, Sport. How's the racing project coming along?"

Brent could not get into it with him right then. "Project?" He shook his head in annoyance. "Yeah, the project is just fine." He headed straight to his bedroom.

Katherine followed him there and closed the door behind her. "Now what, Brent? What did I do wrong this time?"

Brent sat on the edge of his bed. "Every time I turn around that guy is moving in on me...taking my place."

Katherine sat down beside him and stroked his hair. "Bobby is not taking your place. No one in this world will ever take your place. How can I convince you of that?"

"Mom, I think you and I need to take a time out. I'll be going away for a while with Uncle Martin and Mac. We're taking the Avenger on the road with the National series and it'll mean a lot of traveling."

She dropped her hands to her lap and lowered her head. "You're running out on me." A tear formed in the corner of her eyes. "Honey, I am trying to put my life...our lives, back together and I understand how hard this is for you. I asked you before to stand with me on this. We need each other."

"Mother." He seldom called her Mother. "There is stuff going on in both our lives right now we have to take care of. A time out may be a way for that to happen."

"What is going on in your life that you have to leave me out?"

"Mom, when Dad died I stayed with Uncle Martin and Aunt Suz for the summer. That allowed you time to sort out some things. You're still sorting. Now, I need that same time."

"Time for what, Son?"

"Time for me."

She wiped a tear from her cheek. "It hurts me to say this, but you're probably right." She wiped her cheek again. "I never promised it would be easy, but I do promise we will get through this. We have to play the cards life deals us, Brent. Our only control is which cards to keep and which ones to throw away. Hopefully, we make the right choices. Just don't make it sound like goodbye."

Brent fidgeted on the bed. "It's not goodbye, Mom. It's more like, I'll see you later."

They hugged until the mood softened, then Katherine whispered, "Okay. I'll talk to Marty." She placed her chin on the top of his head. "You will keep me informed regularly."

He wasn't sure if it was a question or a command. It didn't matter. "Of course! And likewise about you and…well, you know…him."

She laughed lightly. "His name is Robert. And yes, I promise, you will know everything before anything happens."

Brent looked her in the eyes. "And what are you implying may happen?"

She squeezed his hand and then rose and left the room without a reply.

*****

They were back on the road for Somerton Motor Park at 4:30 a.m. Mac loaded two extra Yamaha motors to have as back-ups. "They're used but they're reliable…just in case."

The paddock received additional arrivals since the Avenger team left the previous day. Had the trailer not been parked there overnight, its pit space would have been all the way down near Turn 1 along the chain-link fence.

Both Martin and Brent skipped the warm-up practice, but were suited up and ready to go when the drivers meeting took place.

Martin and Mac went ahead to the meeting while Brent followed a short time later with Nate. Harris Branson was close behind but Hannah was already there talking with another racer.

The meeting was short but direct. After the National Anthem was broadcast, four-cycle sprints lined up on the grid for the first race. Kimmie already had Nate's kart there.

It was a sizeable class with 23 karts entered. Nate ran a strong race and finished third as part of a three kart duel for first place.

Martin's Yamaha Enduro class was the third race. The all-new Avenger stood out from any of the other 28 contestants in the lineup. It held the curiosity of the grid crowd until the one-minute flag cleared them from the area.

Martin shot from tenth place to sixth at the drop of the flag. He was fourth coming out of Turn 1. As the low-slung bullets meandered their way around the twisty elevations, all eyes, even those of the track announcer, were on the "Martin Kessick's Avenger, the newly unveiled Chaparral of karting" as he called it.

As the field strung out, the three leaders kept in a draft by themselves. It took Martin a well executed four laps to break through the formation and take over the lead coming out of the tunnel. By the intensity of cheers and applause, the spectators loved the show. The Avenger set the pace running away for the next two laps.

Brent and Mac were ecstatic. It was clearly the pinnacle for the Avenger marque and for Martin Kessick's return to kart racing.

On Lap 7 he was leading the second place kart by a full three seconds as he barreled into the tunnel. Then 'dah'. The Avenger coasted up the hill and came to a stop on the inside gravel of Turn 5, its engine dead.

The PA speakers rang out the news all through the pits. "The Avenger is off the race track in Turn 5. It appears to have an early finish here today folks." A hush fell over the crowd.

Mac slapped pit wall with his open hand. "Don't tell me!" he yelled with a growl that would shock a grizzly. "Not again!"

Nate stood beside Brent and looked at the ground, shaking his head. Even he felt the frustration.

Brent turned to Mac. "What is going on? How do we stick two motors in as many races?"

Mac slapped pit wall two more times, barely able to speak. "The last two engine builds were with a new supply of circlips. All I can say is they must be a bad batch."

Nate bit on his lip. "Mac, how many motors did you use those circlips on?"

"All the ones we have with us."

Brent's eyes flew open. "What about my new engine, the one Uncle Martin just rebuilt?"

Mac shrugged. "Probably that one too. If he used the new circlips from my parts bin, then your motor is another bomb."

"How fast can we replace them?" Brent demanded.

"The only circlips I have are from the new batch."

Brent threw his arms in the air. "Where am I gonna get a decent motor by race time?"

Mac was still shaking his head in disbelief. "We can swap with the used motors I loaded this morning. Like I said, they're used but they're reliable. And I know they don't have the new circlips in them."

Brent and Nate were across pit road before he even finished his statement. Until Martin got towed in after his race was over, they had the swapped motor on Brent's Avenger and were completing the connections.

Martin was irritated. "Mac, we seem to have a major problem with these motors."

Mac was adjusting the tension of the drive belt. "It's that new set of wrist pin clips we received last week."

"Oh, no!" Martin grumbled. "That means I used them in Brent's engine too."

"We already switched his motor," Mac assured him.

"With what?" Martin asked. "With one of those old ones you loaded up this morning?"

Brent connected the throttle cable. "It's all we have now. We can't afford another stick at this point. Let's hope the term 'old reliable' is accurate."

The PA system crackled. "Yamaha Sprint, you are next on the grid. That's all Yamaha Sprints. Your race goes off in just a few minutes."

"Get geared up," Martin directed. "We'll get your kart to the grid."

Brent's exuberance was as tainted as the partly clouded skies.

CHAPTER 8

AS THE KARTS ARRIVED ON THE GRID they were directed by the steward into their positions, according to their order of registration, along the side of the front straight. The standing start, single file formation angled toward Turn 1. It was fashioned after the legendary Le Mans 24 Hour Endurance Race held annually in France.

Brent was directed into space number 14. As he walked down the line, it was no surprise that he passed the pair of Quantums in the third and fourth spots.

"Early bird gets the worm," he told himself.

Martin arrived moments later pulling the starter dolly with Mac in tow pushing the Avenger.

Track clearance was swift and Brent was in the seat with helmet, gloves and neck brace on before the one-minute-to-flag signal.

Martin knelt beside him ready with the electric starter. "We don't have any data on this motor so we don't know where your carb settings should be. You're on your own this time. Tweak the jets as you see fit."

Mac added, "I believe this motor has about four races on it, so most likely compression is beginning to drop off which will affect top end. So be careful not to run the high jet too lean or you'll stick it for a different reason."

"Got it!"

"And keep alert for my pit board," Martin reminded him. That was a subtle reference to previous times when Brent missed valuable information by not watching for the pit signals.

"Got it!" he repeated.

Flag up. Engines cracked up and down the line and race crews scurried over pit wall. The Avenger fired with one spin of the starter. Considering it was a cold motor, that was encouraging.

Green flag. Exhausts ripped open an already thundering grid.

As those around him lunged across the track dashing for the outside, Brent swung into an opening created along the rail. Like a horde of screaming banshees, the field bore down onto Turn 1.

Three and four abreast snaking around the pond, they exchanged positions like marbles spilling onto the floor. The disorder by Turn 3 had evolved into an unraveling process. Still locked in the middle of it all, Brent continued riding the rail. The carousel ride around the long bend further thinned the congestion. It was after the tunnel, at the start of the incline, that the Avenger fell off pace.

Brent reached over the top of the carburetor and nudged the high speed jet inward. He was passed by two karts while pulling the hill and another one on the back stretch.

A second tweak of the high jet sharpened the

exhaust pitch. *Maybe that will do it*, he hoped.

The Avenger found good grip at the bottom of the hill going into the hairpin and regained the three positions it had lost.

With Turn 11, the esses and the final turn behind him, he went onto the front straight finally feeling some room around him. After the first lap frenzy, he counted nine karts ahead, five directly in front of him and a set of four pulling away. And there was a purple and yellow kart in each group.

The long straight exposed the weak, used motor. Brent expected at least a little more spunk from it. He hoped for a little more spunk from it. In fact, he needed a little more spunk from it. The tachometer only read 13,300. It should have shown at least a thousand rpms more than that.

He gave the jet needle one last small twist. Lean the fuel mixture and get a volatile combustion. Too much and get a disaster. According to the exhaust temperature gauge, he was bordering at the limit.

What the Avenger lacked in top-end speed, it made up for in cornering. It broke into the midst of the five kart pack on the higher terrain of the back course. After the next three bends the Avenger was the pack's new leader. But the conquest was short-lived. By the end of the elevated straightaway, two of the karts slipped past again, one of then being Hannah Branson's.

The two led side-by-side around Turn 9 and down the hill. Under heavy braking for Turn 10, Hannah edged out her opponent and Brent slid into position behind her. He rode up on the Quantum so hard he practically pushed it into the tight left-hander. They rubbed nose against tail through the esses and around Turn 13.

Knowing Hannah had a straightaway advantage

over his tired motor, Brent buried the Avenger in her slipstream so she would tow him along. The effort broke them free from their rivals and closed them up on the foursome ahead.

For three laps they nipped away at the gap separating them from the leaders. Hannah was a smooth driver, precise in her execution and exact on the racing line. Having the opportunity to really study her cornering entry and exit, Brent found it to be flawless. He considered carefully how he would out-maneuver her when the time came to have to do so.

He recalled how Kimmie described her the day before. "She's rich, she's smart, and she's tough." Hannah certainly was all three, with tough being the present peril.

He chose to maintain the draft for the time being, lay back and let her lead. She was getting the job done. After all, with his tired engine, he had very few options.

As she pulled him along, he had a chance to study the habits of the pack ahead. Harrison's Quantum was trapped in the center of it all, jerking from side to side, drilling to get through. He definitely wasn't the smooth, tolerant operator his twin sister was. He was radical and over-zealous. His ambition proved to be more detrimental to the success of the foursome than what it helped them.

On Lap 6 Brent and Hannah caught them, making it a six way duel. That's when Brent received his first pit board message from Martin. 'EZ.'

He signaled that he caught it. EZ. So short and to the point. But why that message? He thought it should be obvious to anyone watching that he was taking it easy. Any easier and he would be out of the lead pack. What did his uncle have in mind?

As instructed, he made no attempt to pass, even though he had an opportunity to overtake Hannah when she got away from the inside on Turn !0. He just hung on at the tail end.

In the tunnel on Lap 10, the six leaders lapped their first two karts, then three more on the backstretch. Their closely knit parade made the passes as smooth and effortless as a train on a set of rails. Only Harris Branson showed any sign of aggressiveness.

Martin signaled with the board again. 'EZ.'

Brent waved again. *Okay*, he thought. *I got it. What's with all the EZs?*

Circling the pond on Lap 14, the parade caught up to the largest group to lap. Harris made a desperate attempt to rectify his stale situation. He strayed from the racing line exiting Turn 3 and rode the long radius on the outside to attempt a bold multiple pass. But with too many karts involved and not enough road, the scene became chaotic. Karts veered in all directions, some outside, some inside, some sideways and one even spun backwards.

Amidst the banging and clipping to his body shell, Brent squeezed into Hannah's push bar. She had slipped into an opening right down the middle and Brent saw it as the only viable option of safely getting through.

When the entourage reached the slight jag of Turn 4, Harris bounced back onto the race track from the gravel shoulder just ahead of Hannah. He wrestled for control through the tunnel and blasted up the hill in the lead, with his sister and Brent in a near collision pursuit.

Daring!

Brent heard the snarling of karts still clearing the ruckus behind him, but he had to focus his attention on the pair ahead. Of all those in the race, the two ahead were the two he would rather have ahead in his sights as opposed to attacking him from behind.

Harris led them erratically through Turns 5 and 6, going in tight and coming out wide. Hannah got under him on Turn 7 forcing him to stay wide.

Brent pressed through with her and entered the backstretch alongside of Harris. Only by working the draft with Hannah could Brent hang even with her brother. His kart didn't have the muscle to do it alone.

Down the hill and entering Turn 10, Brent saw his chance, probably his last chance at Hannah. He remembered Martin's pit board signal, 'EZ,' but he knew now was the time to 'GO.'

Harris was on the inside and Hannah crossed over in front of him. Trapped alone on the outside, Brent dived deep into the curve with all four tires squealing. Confident with the Avenger's superior cornering, he powered through the esses, throttle down, and inched ahead. He cleared Turn 13 and crossed to the inside to stay ahead. He knew his Yamaha was no match on the straight. He had to somehow keep her behind him. Up ahead he saw the flagman poised with the checkered flag in hand.

Then he heard the pitch of another exhaust. Harris was casting a challenge from the right side. The Avenger would not be able to retain him. As colors of purple and yellow invaded his peripheral vision, Brent detected yet another exhaust. Hannah was following through in a draft with her brother.

As the checkered flag grew larger, Harris inched into the lead, pressed hard by Hannah. When they flashed across the finish line, she too had inched ahead of Brent, though just barely.

Harris turned the cool down lap into a showy

victory parade. Flinging his kart from side to side he waved his arms in a circle over his head. Bragging rights belong to the victor and Harrison Branson was just that.

Brent returned to his pit and shut his engine down. Although he was happy not to swallow another DNF, having the taste of victory slip through his lips had a distaste of its own. Third place would not normally be so bad, but giving up the win only yards from the finish line was a hard defeat.

He was greeted heartily by Martin and Mac. Kimmie was even there to greet him.

"When you consider our record lately," Martin rejoiced, "I welcome a third place. Good going there, Buddy."

Brent still had to accept the loss. "We had them covered in the corners. We just didn't have the motor for the straights."

Mac patted him on the shoulder. "We'll take care of that. Your loss on the straights was a poor motor. But your gain in the corners was all kart. You proved we have the kart."

Martin said, "We'll load up, Brent. You go pick up your trophy. At least we have some hardware to show for the weekend."

"I'll walk with you," Kimmie beamed. "It'll be like old times."

Brent got the usual high fives and congratulations along the way. He hoped his thank you returns sounded sincere enough. He couldn't tell. But Kimmie was content sharing the approvals with him.

Hannah had just picked up the first and second place trophies when Brent arrived at the window. It was his first up close encounter with her. She seemed as civil as he thought her to be.

"Thank you for your assistance out there," she smiled. "It helped move us up through that mess." Her smile was bright and genuine.

Brent smiled in return. "Strength comes in numbers. You can accomplish more by working together than you can alone."

There was poetry in her chuckle. "I have tried forever to get my bro to understand that very concept. But he can be stubborn when it comes to competition. It's all about the win to him."

Brent nodded. "I suppose there's a lot of that going around. He reminds me of someone else I encountered a while back."

"Oh, Harris couldn't possibly remind you of anyone else. There is no one like Harrison."

"Yeah, well, he has the compulsive audacity of a Kyle Nash I know."

Hannah's eyes lit up. "I know Kyle Nash. I've seen him around the circuit. He drives one of Quantum's new shifter karts. Harris is nothing like Kyle."

In what context did she mean that? Was it in a good way or a bad way?

The silence that followed was awkward.

Kimmie grabbed Brent's arm to guide him toward the window. "Well, Hannah, it was nice talking to you. Congratulations on your team's performance today. I'm sure we'll see you around."

Hannah smiled again as she turned to leave. "Yes, I'm sure you will."

At the trophy window, Brent turned to look back at her. "She seems like such a nice girl."

Kimmie still had his arm. "That's funny. Isn't that the same thing you thought about me when we met?"

CHAPTER 9

THE NEXT RACE ON THE SCHEDULE was the next weekend at Barrington Springs Speedway. Since it was an eight hour drive, the Avenger team had to be ready to go by the end of the day Wednesday. The road trip itself would absorb most of Thursday, while Friday was needed for Brent and Martin to learn the new track. That meant a short work week at the shop without Martin's assistance. He had to finish up a small construction project under contract before leaving.

Brent spent whatever time he could by preparing both karts with new tires, different gearing and especially new motors. Mac pulled the cylinders off each engine, including the spares, and fitted new wrist pin circlips.

Mid-morning on Thursday found the team rolling up the interstate, hopefully to be better prepared than the last outing. Morale was positive due to Brent's showing at Somerton Motor Park in spite of a used engine.

It was evening until they finally reached the speedway to drop off the trailer. The Barrington facility did not permit camping at the speedway, so all the teams had hotel reservations off-site.

A tunnel beneath the track between Turns 3 and 4 of the oval accessed the infield paddock area. Some race teams arrived early enough in the day to erect canopies. But the crowded infield consisted mostly of locked abandoned trailers.

Martin noticed an empty spot across from the fuel pumps. "This looks like home for the weekend. We'll unhook here and be back to set up in the morning."

Brent looked around for the Quantum trailer. "Just making sure we're not neighbors."

Martin placed a hand on his nephew's shoulder. "Keep in mind there are others we race against besides the Bransons."

Brent grunted. "Sometimes I wonder."

Martin tightened his grip. "There's no wondering about it. You have to get Branson out of your mind and think ahead...and I'm talking about both Bransons."

"They always seem to gang up on me, that's all. And Harris is ruthless."

"But stop fretting over it," Martin continued. "Get him off your mind. Don't let him beat you before you even hit the race track."

"I know, you told me that before."

Martin let go of his shoulder. "I'd like to think I *taught* you that before."

When they returned Friday morning, the infield was hopping with activity. Teams were busy preparing their pit area. Racers were busy preparing their kart. Track officials were busy preparing for a weekend of racing. The PA system gurgled all morning with instructions and information. The mood throughout the facility was all action.

Following safety tech and a brief drivers meeting,

the track opened for sprint practice and Brent was set to go. He was growing more comfortable with the Avenger and confident with his new motor. His focus once again was to learn this new track. Since Nate had not made the trip and he didn't have another driver for guidance, he was on his own. He rummaged through his memory for his uncle's tips of interpreting a new race course.

He paced himself with the others for the first two laps to get his thoughts aligned. Barrington Springs Speedway was a 1½ mile banked stock car oval with an added ¾ mile, flat infield road course. The wide banked oval mixed with the narrow, tighter infield course made an interesting layout.

Turn 1 was at the end of pit road. It transitioned from oval to road course directly from the front straightaway. Turn 2 formed a dogleg that headed back toward the pits. Turn 3 was the common hairpin with Turns 4 and 5 being classic right-handers. A very short connecting straight fed Turns 6, 7 and the esses. Turn 8 rejoined the oval 100 yards down track from Turn 1.

The high speed banking began with Turn 9 but leveled off for the widest and longest backstretch. Because Turns 10 and 11 were connected banked turns, they resembled a bowl. The start-finish line was beyond the midpoint of the front straight to embrace a dash to the finish. It was a different kind of race track for Brent, but one he felt he could adjust to with ease.

For the remainder of the practice session, Brent settled in and began analyzing the circuit. Due to the banking, the oval portion was pretty straight forward, mostly all throttle. But because of the tight corners and reduced road width, he considered the infield portion to be a one groove race track. Passing there would require diligence.

The end of practice was flagged from Turn 11 to divert racers directly onto pit road and avoid a lengthy cool down lap. When Brent returned to the pit, Martin was anxiously waiting to take his turn with the enduro.

"It's a smooth run," Brent reported. "It's all throttle on the oval and a delicate mix on the road course. Except for the banking on the oval, it is pancake flat."

Martin fastened his helmet. "It should be a quick learn then. How did the motor feel?"

"I didn't push it yet. I'll let you know the next time out."

Brent watched the practice from pit wall. It was at about the halfway point that he saw the Branson twins arrive with their karts and park in a pit space beside the Avenger.

"Looks like I'll have company in my next practice," he told Mac.

Mac nodded. "Yeah, I see. Hide your cards. Fool them into thinking they have the set-up. Always keep an ace up your sleeve."

"I know," Brent acknowledged. "Don't beat them in practice. Beat them in the race."

"You're catching on," Mac grinned.

Harris stood beside his Quantum and carefully scrutinized the Avenger's unorthodox molded construction. Brent stepped away from the trackside pit wall to confront him.

Mac grabbed him by the arm. "Hold on, Brent. Let him feast his eyes. We have nothing to hide. His curiosity is a good thing."

Brent stopped. "If I see him touch my kart, I'll tear his face off."

Mac let go of his arm and laughed. "Boy, you do have it bad with that guy."

When the enduros completed their session, Martin returned to the pit and joined Mac and Brent at trackside to watch the shifter karts practice. The 125cc, six-speed, water-cooled racers were small Indy car replicas, fast and powerful.

Brent spotted his former nemesis, Kyle Nash, among the foray. Feeling edgy, his attention was divided between the karts on the racetrack and the couple on pit lane behind him.

He finally had to go back to where the Avenger sat alone along the armor rail. Harris was seated in his Quantum and purposely avoided eye contact with Brent. Hannah was standing next to him straddling her own kart.

"Good morning," she greeted when Brent knelt to retrieve his helmet and neck brace.

"Hi," he returned, trying not to sound too perky.

"Where is your girlfriend this morning?"

Brent delayed pulling on his helmet. "I don't have a girlfriend."

Hannah acted surprised, though the slight trace of a smile showed. "The little red-haired girl I see you with?"

Brent matted his fluffy hair for the helmet. "Oh, Kimmie! Well, she is a girl…and she is a friend."

Hannah's smile widened as she settled into her seat. "Hey, maybe we'll get to run together again in the race tomorrow."

Harris mumbled just loud enough to be heard, "If that contraption will stay running."

A bolt of heat raced through Brent's blood.

"Stop it Harris!" Hannah ordered. She looked up at Brent with her large round eyes. "Good luck this weekend."

Brent bit down on his lower lip. "Yeah, you too."

At the flag, Harris tore away as usual, always having to place himself in front of everyone else, even in practice. Remembering Mac's advice, Brent allowed Hannah to get away from him also. He didn't want to tangle with them, at least not yet.

Maintaining a safe distance from the Bransons, he let the kart wind all the way up to peak rpms on the oval, and pushed it harder and deeper in the corners. It felt good. It responded vigorously. It was as aggressive as any of the competition surrounding it.

Halfway through the practice, he unknowingly pulled within sight distance of the Bransons. Remembering Mac's advice, he eased up and re-established the gap between them. *Don't beat them in practice*, he reminded himself. Then he recalled even Kimmie suggested he lay low with them. Or was she referring only to Hannah?

Even sandbagging it, the Avenger out-performed the competition. Brent kept the Bransons in his sight as they proceeded to slice through the field ahead. If they stayed with their present set-up, Brent definitely held the ace up his sleeve Mac had mentioned.

When he returned to the pits, Mac directed him to a spot away from the Bransons. He looked annoyed.

Brent got out of his seat. "What's the matter?"

"I told you not to show your hand out there."

"I let them go ahead of me like you wanted so we wouldn't run together."

Mac shook his head. "But then you ran them down like you had something to prove."

Brent shrugged. "I stayed behind them so they wouldn't see me."

"But their team saw you. And they had a stopwatch on you. You may have thought you were invisible, but they timed you the whole time you were out there."

Brent sighed. "Mac, we have them in the bag."

"Don't bet on it anymore," Mac replied. "You don't know how bad you showed them up. They're probably re-gearing as we speak."

"It was just their warm-up run," Brent defended. "They were probably sandbagging too."

Mac looked him square in the eye. "You're talking about Harrison Branson. He is all show, all go, all the time. Sandbagging isn't in his vocabulary."

The reality of Mac's statement sent Brent's ego backpedaling into anguish.

CHAPTER 10

SATURDAY'S WEATHER AS IT WAS forecast on Friday proved to be right on; hazy, hot and humid. After a night at a nearby hotel, the Avenger team arrived at the track early, or so they thought. The mood in the pits was like practice day on steroids. Not only was every pit space taken, but karts had invaded the grass strip along the back fence. Even the grandstand showed a steady migration of fans that early. A few spectators with pit passes roamed the infield to mingle among the drivers and karts.

Brent was mixing a fresh batch of racing fuel when a voice interrupted his concentration. "Good morning!"

"Hi," Brent said without looking up. "I didn't realize anyone was here."

"You were so absorbed in your work. I suppose you'll always be that precision minded."

"Pretty much," Brent replied as he finally looked up. "What can I do for…?"

Standing beside the Avenger with her boyfriend

Kyle Nash, was Alexa Jolene Barlett, an acquaintance from his racing past. A.J. was his co-driver in the Silva 3 Hour Endurance race two years ago. Her father, Les, had been part of their pit crew. Brent abruptly dropped his funnel and hugged her.

"I keep hearing about you, Brent," she said. "You never cease to amaze me." She studied his kart. "Avenger. Very impressive. I thought I'd get a close-up and personal look if you don't mind."

Brent backed up to check her over. She was still the looker he remembered her to be, those light blue eyes and golden complexion. "How have you been, A.J.? Are you still racing?"

She chuckled. "Oh my no, only at heart. Daddy isn't doing real well right now so we put my racing on hold. For now I attend whatever races I can with Kyle, mainly his shifter kart races."

Brent relaxed. "So, you say you keep hearing about me. I was hoping to be a little more inconspicuous for a while longer."

"Well then I have to tell you, Brent Lockeman, I'm sorry, but you will never be inconspicuous."

Then a familiar voice chimed in. "No he won't." Hannah Branson just joined the conversation. She turned to Kyle. "Nice to see you again, Kyle."

Kyle gave her a cozy hug. "Hello, Hannah. You look charming as always."

She gave him a playful nudge in the rib. "You need a new line there Nash. That one hasn't worked for you yet." She winked at A.J.

Kyle returned the banter. "Hey, I blame that more on Harrison than I do on you."

"My brother is getting to be quite a thorn with you boys. You know he's only being protective."

"You mean controlling, Hannah. You don't need protection."

"True, Kyle." she concurred. "But it's comforting nevertheless."

Brent had to weigh in on the subject, "I have to agree with Kyle on that one, Hannah. You don't need protection." Then he gulped. He couldn't believe he just blurted it out like that.

Hannah was about to comment when Martin emerged from the trailer. "Brent, we decided to run the harder tires…" He stopped when he saw the three guests. "Well, my oh my. A.J. it's been a long time. It is really good to see you. Say hello to your father for me." Then he recognized the other guests. "And a good morning to you too, Miss Branson. How are you today?"

"Hi," Hannah beamed. "I'm fine thank you. I was just on my way past and I saw Kyle here. Have a safe race today, all of you."

"Thank you," Martin replied. "And the same to you."

The moment then felt a little awkward.

"Well, I have to run along," Hannah waved. "Bye."

Kyle and A.J. gave a nod of farewell also and stepped onto pit road behind her.

"What was that all about?" Martin asked when they were out of earshot.

"I'm not sure, Uncle Martin. It was just spontaneous."

When the track opened, both Bransons ran the short practice. Harris made it a point to dominate, letting everyone in attendance know he was there.

In the enduro practice, Martin took a couple of laps to test the tire change. Satisfied with the decision to run a harder compound tire, he returned to the pit and directed Brent to switch over also.

Mac returned from trackside with a stopwatch report. He looked grim. "Harris has a half second lead on Brent."

Brent shrugged. "I was holding back yesterday, remember? We have him in the bag."

Mac grunted. "Maybe Harris is holding back too." He paused. "You never, ever, have the race in the bag before it starts. Remember that. I've seen races lost right on the very last turn."

"Heck," Martin corrected. "I've seen them lost on the very first turn."

Martin's lay-down class was the second race on the schedule. At 45 minutes in length, the front seven runners made it a real crowd pleaser. The multiple lead changes with tight, clean, close racing kept the spectators on edge. Martin was in that front pack until two laps from the end. He happened to be leading at the time when another racer nudged him entering the esses and he hooked a rear wheel off the edge of the pavement. The Avenger dropped onto the robust axle clutch, stripping the toothed drive belt from the gearing.

Martin coasted onto the infield grass, his second DNF in as many races. The Avenger Enduro's unveiling was less than successful. Mac and Brent were waiting at the weigh-in scales when the tow rig dropped it off after the roundup.

The lines of concern on Martin's face were dreadful. "Two more laps," he winched. "Just two more laps and we'd have chalked up our first victory."

Brent understood Mac's silence. He heard in his soul what Mac wasn't saying. It had been said already, earlier that very day. *You never have it in the bag until it's over.*

During the time leading up to Brent's race, he diligently went over the kart, confirming the clutch setting, brake adjustment and tire pressures. He checked and double-checked all fasteners, brake lines and fuel lines. Never before was it more evident to him that despite the utmost preparation in racing, any number of circumstances could put him out of contention. Victory is never in the bag until the race is over.

The mood that shrouded Team Avenger was somber. There were no last minute words of encouragement or instruction from Martin on the grid, only silence. With starter in hand, there was only silence.

Right from the drop of the green flag, Brent shot from tenth place to seventh before Turn 1. By the esses he had captured the fifth spot, and by the time the class got around to the high speed oval, he had joined the four karts in the front pack. He could see Harrison holding down the number two position up ahead, but he couldn't see how far Hannah was behind him.

Then he remembered what Martin advised him earlier, that there were competitors other than the Bransons to contend with. So why was he constantly gauging everything by them? Why should it matter where Hannah Branson was? *Concentrate on what is ahead, not behind,* he was always told.

Suddenly it registered. That was the problem. Harrison Branson was up ahead. Harrison would be the major obstacle for him to overcome. That Quantum was becoming the thorn in his side.

His conjecture came to life on Lap 3. While preserving his position at the tail end of the lead pack, he glided onto the oval banking from Turn 8 only to catch a flash of purple and yellow on his right. Hannah was challenging for his position.

"So much for not worrying who or what is behind," he said under his breath.

Side by side on the bowl, they spilled onto the long backstretch. Brent held his inside line. If Hannah wanted it, she would have to earn it by her own gusto.

Entering the banking of Turn 10, the fourth place kart ahead dropped to the flat lane, deep inside. Brent swung to his left, half on the flat lane, and half on the slope. Hannah slipped into the higher groove above, making it three abreast.

Turn 11 was the same order. Brent wrestled to maintain balance between the flat lane and the banking as he fought the inertia fed, navigational over-steer.

Down the front straightaway, the trio shared fourth place. But Hannah was in the slipstream of the third place kart and crept ahead.

Brent dismally tucked in behind her to follow. By the start-finish line the pair had overtaken the third place kart and rolled up alongside the other Quantum.

They lunged from the oval into Turn 1 to cross behind the pits. There Brent got his first good look at the leader, none other than the taped-up apparatus of the Colton boy. And he conducted quite a smooth, sweeping transition onto the road course. Apparently, the crude machine was as fast as Kimmie said it was.

But a smooth transition or not, the narrowed cartway feeding Turn 2 pinched Brent toward Harris. Hannah got through, leaving Brent and Harris in a hub-to-hub match-up for third place going into the hairpin.

Brent held the inside. As Harris attempted to regain the groove, he over compensated and the Quantum broke traction.

The first bang was the Quantum's nose slamming

into the Avenger's front wing. The second and stronger bang, which resonated all through Brent's body, was the Quantum's front hub following through.

Locked together, the two karts launched onto the infield in a bee-line toward Turn 4. Neither driver lifted from the throttle. Ignoring the waving yellow flag, they diced across the grass and hopped back on the track in the middle of the turn.

Hannah and the Colton boy were halfway to Turn 5. But by the time Brent and Harris got to the turn, a black flag was waving them both into the pits.

The mandated reduced speed was punishing to Brent. He followed Harris along the edge of the roadway as the other racers sped past him, still racing. He was given the reminder black flag at each station along the way, while a rolled yellow flag followed his progress to alert the others. Adding to his torment was a sense of a vibration in the Avenger that wasn't there before it was broadsided.

Race officials were waiting at the tower when the two adversaries arrived. But Harris wasn't waiting for them. He no sooner shut his kart down than he charged at Brent, fists clenched. Two officials restrained him as Brent bounded from the Avenger in self-defense.

"I swear, you need to be banned from racing," Harris shouted as he struggled against his suppressers.

"You rammed me, Moron," Brent yelled as he too was restrained.

The race director slipped between them. "I think it's time you two boys take a serious hiatus. You've developed quite a history together." His voice was gruff and confirmed his authority. "You're finished for this event. Both of you...pack it up."

The crowd formed a closed ring around the

charged scene. Harris flung his arms and legs in protest, still trying to get free. "You're going down, Lockeman…you got that jerk? You're going down!"

Brent was equally charged. "Bring it bonehead, any time, anywhere!"

At that moment Harris broke free and with a wild swing, landed a fist into Brent's cheek.

Drawing on every ounce of fight in him, Brent still could not get a punch of his own off. His arms were shackled by two men and his torso by the stronghold of another. He stared down at Harris, who by then was taken to the ground.

Silence prevailed. When his captors relaxed their hold, Brent pointed his finger at Harrison. "You just bought yourself a payback…guaranteed. Be watching for it!"

As he turned away, he saw his old friends, A.J. Barlett and Kyle Nash. A.J. looked somber. Kyle smiled in an attempt to calm Brent. "I'm glad to see you still have that old fire in you, Lockeman. Welcome to the Nationals."

The eight hour drive home was long, depressing and silent.

CHAPTER 11

THE AVENGER HAD TAKEN A HARD, solid hit on the left side. A quick inspection in the shop on the stand showed a bent spindle and a dented wheel hub. A broken nose wing and an arched tie rod completed the list of damages.

"Our spare parts inventory is getting low," Mac reported. "And this molded wing is going to be meticulous to repair. It's time to get serious about a sponsor." He scratched his head. "That must have been some blow."

"It was," Brent huffed. "Believe me, it was. And I owe Harris one."

Martin leaned against the workbench with his arms crossed. "Are you sure you're alright?"

"I'm fine. I just owe that Branson moron a facial."

Martin looked at the floor shaking his head. "That's the second time you said that. I have to keep telling you, there can be no grudges on the race track. Now, let it go."

With animosity in his voice, Brent replied, "I promise, Uncle Martin, payback won't happen on the track."

Martin was stern. "That squirmish got both of you tossed out of the race yesterday. If this happens again, you'll be out for the season. Where would that leave Avenger Racing?"

"I'm sorry, Uncle Martin," Brent argued. "But that conceited jerk needs to be stopped before somebody gets hurt."

"Don't make it your business to be that someone." Martin advised. "You will always have a Harrison Branson to deal with in the world. Be Brent Lockeman. It will take you so much farther."

Mac quietly stood beside the Avenger until Martin finished. "Well then, now that the lessons of life are over with, let's talk about how much further Avenger Racing is going. This is zero-for-two gentlemen. We have some fabrication to tend to before we see a race track again. We have parts to purchase and hours of labor to cover."

"We'll get it done, Mac," Martin assured. "Okay, so we have some issues plaguing us besides design and development, but we'll get it done."

"It's just that we're running low on the finances," Mac stated frankly. "A racing effort takes design and development, yes. But it takes money too. We have to sell karts to make money and we have to win races to sell karts." His jaw tightened as he contemplated his next statement. "And we have to finish races in order to win races."

Brent was speechless as he stared into the solemn faces of his two elders. This was a quandary all too new to him, a predicament he never had to consider before. "What do you mean we're running out of money?" It came out as a low murmur.

Martin was still leaning against the workbench with his arms crossed. "In the current economy, Brent, the building industry has taken a big hit. There aren't many good paying construction projects out there. That is what always financed my racing hobby. You know the score; you have to pay to play."

"Mac," Brent pleaded. "You always had this covered...didn't you?"

Mac looked away before answering. "Brent, the Avenger is an expensive undertaking. This shop needs fed. All the materials and components need income to support them. Selling karts was to be that support. We got it going alright but now we have to prove to the racing world that it's worthy of keeping it going. Unfortunately, the hardware industry is like the construction business right now...down."

No one spoke for a couple of minutes, a long, painful couple of minutes. Brent sensed the calm that precedes the storm. Then he asked softly, "Are you saying Avenger Racing is finished?"

"No," Martin replied. "Not exactly...not yet anyway. But we have to be logical. As much as we enjoy racing, we need the funds to keep going. If the Avenger won't stand on its own merit we need sponsors to chip in. We need financial resources."

"For now we plan to continue on the national circuit," Mac insisted. "At least for a few more races. But we have to get into the black with this or we won't be able to continue."

Brent grappled to hold on to his dream. "Kimmie's friend Nate builds motors for other racers. It helps pay the bills. It keeps him racing."

Mac nodded. "Nate Cormick's engines win races.

Ours stick from bad circlips."

"Come on! You guys build good engines, too," Brent argued. "I know you do because I've had them. We can be a jobber for other racers at the track, and supply parts and service."

"We need a platform," Martin said. "We have to create a platform to launch the Avenger. The Southern Grand Prix at the Heartland Motor Speedway is hosting a karting extravaganza in conjunction with their annual sports car event. Imagine the platform it would give us with that kind of exposure."

Mac grunted. "Yeah, but getting another 'also ran' on our record will seal our coffin for good. I'd feel better knowing we at least had a decent chance to prove ourselves."

Brent's heart pounded, ecstatic at the opportunity just mentioned, yet confused by the uncertainty cast over the Avenger. "When have we shied away from a challenge before? I face the uncertainty every time I sit on the starting grid. The Southern Grand Prix sounds like the boost we need. Are we any worse off not to try it?"

Martin began to laugh. "Brent, I have to give you this...you are the genuine optimist. Even when you're down, you give looming defeat one last kick of fury."

"I wonder where he gets that from," Mac jested. "Seems to me he's got a little of his uncle's blood in him."

Martin pushed away from the bench. "Okay, we've proven the Avenger to ourselves. What we need is a pair of killer motors. Rocky Point is next on the schedule in two weeks. The Southern GP is after that. Mac, you give both karts a total go-over. I'll build us a pair of destroyer engines. It's time we step up or shut up."

Brent's face lit up for the first time in days. "What do you need me to do?"

Mac nodded toward the service bay up front. "You handle the service work out there. We'll take care of the Avengers back here."

The engine was off both karts and on the workbench before another word was uttered. Both chassis were on sawhorses to be reworked and fine-tuned. Mac prepared a parts list of engine components he didn't have in his inventory. That list was placed on order the next day along with two complete Yamaha 100 motors. He wasn't going to risk anything to chance with the new motors. Martin would blueprint them both to his own personal specifications.

The following week, Mac re-aligned the Avenger sprint's front end and fabricated new spindles from his remaining stock. He also rebuilt both axle clutches with new discs and tungsten weights. He was temporarily pulled off the project to perform cylinder work on a pair of chainsaws brought in by a prime customer, but stayed on the Avengers otherwise.

Brent handled all the scheduled maintenance work and walk-in requests along with another employee. Hopefully with a financial partner for Avenger Racing, Mac's L&M Hardware store would remain viable.

Most of Martin's days consisted of finishing a remodeling job he had contracted to do. But his evenings found him in the back shop meticulously building the pair of racing motors. Every successful racing effort depended on extraordinary driving, a superb vehicle and a top-notch engine. Martin was determined to do his part to provide all three.

Brent quietly observed as his uncle strived to provide that top-notch engine factor. He trued the case alignment, milled the heads, trimmed the piston skirts and cc'd the cylinder heads of both motors. Although every engine running in their classes were the same, it was the attention to detail that separated the winner from second place.

As he witnessed the precision going into each motor, he couldn't shake the images of the Branson Quantums regularly stealing the checkered flag. Stealing it or earning it, Brent struggled with the interpretation. But whichever it was, he was determined...Harris Branson had to be taken down.

CHAPTER 12

ROCKY POINT SPEEDWAY WAS A SIX hour drive through picturesque mountains. The views across the valleys were spectacular. Though wide and smooth, the interstate highway was laden with sweeping curves and elevation changes. The truck rolled along with ease around the ravines and embankments in spite of overcast skies and intermittent showers. The mood in the cab was enthusiastic, with freshened up karts, new top-tier motors and a pair of charged-up drivers. Avenger Racing was as prepared for the next encounter as it could ever be.

They arrived at a sparsely attended paddock in the early evening. The inclement weather held such a damper over the speedway, that the dozen or so trailers present were locked up and abandoned. Everybody would be in one of only three area hotels, which were five miles away in the lower elevations.

The tiny remote settlement of Rocky Point consisted of exactly three hotels, four restaurants, one surprisingly active night club and a gasoline station. Car, motorcycle and kart racing programs were held there weekly from early March through late October. Commerce generated from the participants and spectators of the speedway accounted for 85% of the local economy. Actually, as rumor had it, the few commercial enterprises there were in essence a supporting arm of the racing activity.

The night club, with billboard advertising up and down the interstate, was like an entertainment oasis in the highlands. Secondary to the speedway, it was the entertainment.

Mac, Martin and Brent enjoyed a nice meal of steak and seafood at the diner beside their hotel, and settled in for the night.

"The gates open at 6:30 tomorrow," Martin read from the registration packet. "Sprint practice kicks off at 7:30. Brent, you should be ready to roll for that first round. It may be sparse that early so you should have some good track time. We both have to break in our motors and study this track."

Brent thought for a moment. "Do you want to risk an early practice on a wet track?"

"The track crew will be out early drying the track," Martin replied. "Take it slow. It'll be perfect for seating the new piston rings."

As they walked across the parking lot to return to the hotel, Brent noticed all the trucks that arrived in the meantime. Music from the night club across the road had invaded the tiny settlement also. That parking lot was filling up even faster than the hotel's.

A long line awaited them at the speedway gate the next morning. New arrivals doubled the number that was there the night before. It was after 7 o'clock when Mac finally unlocked the trailer door and began setting up their pit. Martin wheeled the two karts into view as Brent prepared a jug of racing fuel for the day. Heads turned for a glimpse of the new marque but no one approached them.

Practice was delayed until 8:00 since the track crew didn't have it quite ready, which gave Mac and Martin time to erect the canopy.

The clouds were still heavy when the PA system announced an open track for all sprint karts, but the skies were thinning. It was forecast to be cloudy all day but with no rain.

"Watch your exhaust temp," Martin advised. "The air is heavy so your mixture may be too lean already. Run the carb a little rich to seat the rings."

Mac added, "And the track is fresh, no groove put down yet. Just ride around, settle down, and bring it back here in one piece."

"Thank you, my trusted guru," Brent grinned sarcastically. "What would I ever do without you?"

Mac huffed. "I keep wondering that myself."

Eight karts took to the track with Brent, but only one of them was a fellow Yamaha. The rest were in Heavy, Four-cycle and Controlled classes. Brent settled in as advised and let the other Yamaha run off with a trio up ahead. An empty track was exactly what he needed to cure a new motor and check out a new course.

Turn 1 was a long radius hairpin, to the right, but wide and faster than usual. After a short straight, Turn 2 hooked sharply to the left. Whatever momentum was carried through the hairpin would then be lost. From there it was uphill to a mirror image Turn 3, hooking sharply to the right. The ½ mile long, elevated backstretch reminded Brent of the highway that got him to Rocky Point only a day before. A strip of safety run-off area separated the guardrailed drop-off similar to the highway. Turn 3 would be a clean shot onto the backstretch if not interrupted by a slight chicane called Turn 4.

Brent glided along the inside edge and checked his gauges. The engine temperature was low while the new piston ring seated itself, and that was expected.

At the end of the straightaway was a tight double-back to the right. Turn 5 began the descent from the plateau. Turns 6, 7 and 8 combined to form a fast set of downhill esses. They landed at the bottom in an acute, left-handed Turn 9. Turn 10 came without warning around the back of an embankment which funneled into the right-handed and final Turn 11.

With the throttle opened on the ¾ mile main straight, the engine temperature settled into a comfortable range. Brent saluted an 'all clear' to Mac and Martin as he passed the start-finish line and embarked on his next lap.

Avenger negotiated the circuit smoothly but the engine was still trying to come to life. With the elevation changes and sharp corners, another lap would reveal much. Although a couple more karts had joined the session, Brent had little concern. He had more important matters to concentrate on.

He stayed out on the track, cruising unaccompanied, until the checkered flag ended the practice. He avoided anything that would draw attention or show his hand. He hoped to achieve that in due time.

Martin was set to take the enduro out when Brent returned. "That looked smooth enough from the sidelines. What was it like from the driver's seat?"

Brent dropped his helmet and gloves on the seat. "This place has some tight corners. It's like a sprint track with long straightaways. And there are a few double-backs that sneak up on you."

Mac listened to the description. "Be thinking about gear ratios, Marty. We may have to experiment."

The loud speaker blared with static. "The track is now open for enduros. All enduro karts…you're up."

"See you guys shortly," Martin waved as he shoe-horned himself into the reclined seat.

Brent joined Mac along pit wall after giving his uncle a start. He was surprised at how many karts filed into the paddock area during his practice run. But his eyes were peeled for one kart in particular, a purple and yellow one.

"I haven't seen them yet," Mac said.

"Seen who?" Brent asked on impulse.

Mac chuckled. "You know who, a certain tall, slim twin. She's written all over your face."

Brent blushed. "Knock it off. I just happened to notice how filled up pit road has gotten."

"Yeah, okay," Mac's response was drowned out by the first group of karts speeding past.

Like Brent, Martin also chose to run the full practice. He hung with three other karts that seemed to be sandbagging as well. He flashed a hand signal when he passed that everything was okay. The motor sounded healthy amidst the ring-ding of the other three in his group. Not having the deep throaty twang it should confirmed it wasn't yet seated in.

When he returned to the pit, Martin pulled a cold drink from the cooler. He motioned for Brent's attention. "You can pretty much eliminate Turn 4 altogether if you late apex on 3 and dump directly onto the straightaway. The alignment is perfect for it. It feels unsure at first but the track comes back to you if you stay on the throttle. Try it the next time. Treat the kink like it isn't there."

"What's your take on our new spindle degree?" Mac asked.

"Not sure yet. I have to push it deeper into those tight double-backs Brent talked about. But this a track that would warrant those adjustable spindles you've been thinking about."

"I want them ready for the Southern Grand Prix," Mac affirmed. "They may be a bit pricey but it will eliminate the need to stock various sets."

The raspy shifter karts launched from the hot pit for their first practice of the weekend. They left as one huge mass with a thunderous roar. Brent shook his head as he tried to imagine the G-forces they must exert.

At that moment he noticed the Quantum trailer glide along the far end of the paddock. The Bransons had arrived. Something inside him had been hoping they wouldn't show. Yet strangely, something inside him was glad they did.

CHAPTER 13

A TRADITION OF THE NATIONAL
Endurance Series is to offer a special practice session for
novice drivers, those new racers who could benefit from
their own, separate 'learning' practice. It spared them the
first time congestion with the seasoned racers. The
novice practice followed the shifter practice, then the
morning resumed with the regular schedule.

Brent had the Avenger on the pre-grid when the
novices cleared the raceway. There was no sign of the
Quantums on the grid; however, he did see the region's
very own hero, the taped-up, multi-colored kart of the
local Colton brothers.

Brent decided to pick up the pace and it was
obvious his competition did as well. He let the rpms top
out on the straights, and pushed deeper into the corners.
Still careful not to over accelerate coming off the turns, he
preserved the Yamaha's bottom end. It needed one more
heat cycle to cure the rebuild and allow full range of
torque and throttle the next time out.

He made mental notes of his braking and turn-in points for each corner. He noticed the change in the Avenger's attitude as he pushed it more. Its slight over-steer became more pronounced, more aggressive. It delivered more bite to the tires.

The competition became more aggressive too. Drivers got more acclimated to the track and their kart, more daring and less cautious.

The downhill run through the esses brought an increase of contact and spins. By mid practice, one kart had already over-shot the backstretch and hurtled 20 yards off course. Two others connected at the bottom of the hill and never made it to Turn 9.

Brent planted the Avenger squarely on the racing line as he circled the course. Once he mastered the apex, he found Martin's advice on the Turn 4 chicane to be right on. Exit Turn 3 correctly and he could skim right through Turn 4. It also provided a charge onto the straight with an additional 500 rpms. It was a good call, further proof that Uncle Martin knew how to read a track.

From the scrutiny of the roaming spectators as he rolled down pit road, Brent realized the Avenger was no longer inconspicuous. "I was hoping we wouldn't be noticed quite this soon," he told Martin when he stepped from the kart.

"You can blame the announcer for that," Martin frowned. "He mentioned you all throughout the session. I guess we're public now. Keep your cool and don't let it get to you. We'll do our racing when the race comes."

Martin sat out his next practice so they could change all their tires to a harder compound while Mac slipped the clutch engagements a couple hundred rpms. The temperature had risen into the upper 80s, and they had to adjust accordingly. The blanket of thin clouds on a practice day kept the grandstands sparse. But the pits were in full bustle getting set-ups dialed in.

When Brent arrived at the grid for his next practice, Hannah greeted him. "Your new kart is getting some attention. I keep hearing your name mentioned over and over."

Brent frowned. "I was hoping to blend in and not call attention."

Her smile complemented her bob hair and smooth complexion. "You should know better than that. When a new team joins the circuit with something like you have, it's sure to make the buzz."

Harris interrupted. "Come on, Sis. I need you to give me a start." He didn't look at Brent.

Hannah turned to follow her brother and then looked back. "Bye, and I won't tell anyone your secret."

"What secret?"

"Shh." She touched her index finger to her lips and winked.

Brent still pondered what that was all about when Martin joined him by the kart. "Well, I see you finally got your much awaited greeting. Now that you got that out of the way, you can get your mind back to the task at hand."

Brent fastened his helmet strap. "What is it that everyone's thinking?"

Martin laughed and handed him his neck brace and gloves. "Brent, Brent, Brent," was all he said.

A full harvest of sprinters was on the track for the next round of practice. There were karts running in every corner. Brent worked the Avenger hard in all the turns but stayed conservative on the straights to conceal his top end. He still hoped for some level of obscurity but as Hannah pointed out, the buzz had already been made.

He couldn't determine exactly which karts on the track were in his class. He could distinguish the four-strokes and the two-cycle Heavies, but that still left a slew of others. He knew without a doubt the pair of Quantums and the Colton contraption were in his class. For that reason, he avoided them. He didn't want to give them any indication of what the Avenger could do. In fact, they probably knew too much already.

Lap after lap he kept one eye on the racing line and one on his formidable rivals. He braked and turned-in on cue, bringing the touch to a fine impulse. Rocky Point Speedway would have to be second nature to him if he was to perform top-notch. The course would have to become instinct.

Martin was already on the pre-grid when Brent returned, so he parked the Avenger under the canopy, grabbed a cold drink and went to the grid. The round-up crew was towing in the breakdowns.

"We had a clock on you," Mac informed him. "Do you think you were dragging by two seconds?"

Brent sipped from his drink. "At least. I may even be good for three seconds."

"Good, because that's what it will take to run with the Quantums."

Martin looked up from his bed in the enduro. "Just so you know, Brent, the Branson camp had a watch on you too."

Brent grinned. "So they're worried."

"At least they're interested," Mac said.

Brent stayed with Mac at trackside to evaluate Martin's competition. The stopwatch showed comparable times to three other karts chosen at random. Martin was smooth and quite relaxed behind the wheel, a testament to his former championship days. But by the dull exhaust note, Brent could tell the Avenger was harboring some power in reserve. Martin wasn't winding it up to its peak.

When Martin returned after his full run, he proposed a notion...forego the remainder of practice. "There are only two more rounds to go, but I believe we're ready. We have everyone studying us now. It's time to close up shop."

"That suits me," Brent agreed. "Why risk something?"

It didn't take long to roll the two Avengers into the trailer and pack away the fuel and tires. Brent stepped from around the trailer after removing his driver suit.

"You're leaving already?" The voice was soft and comforting.

It took him by surprise. "Hi, Hannah," he responded. "Yeah, we're calling it quits for the day."

"Too bad. I was looking forward to running with you one of these rounds. We'll miss you out there."

Brent tightened his jaw. "I hear you were timing me."

"Bro checks out all his competition. He's paranoid like that."

Brent turned away. "Tell Bro his competition just checked out then."

"You two boys have to stop letting the other bother you. He's way too competitive, and you're too sensitive. If you would both ease up just a little, you would see you're very much alike."

Brent huffed. "I'm not sure I'd want to know that."

Her thin smile never wavered. "Oh, but I think I would." She bid a civil farewell. "I'll see you tomorrow."

The afternoon consisted of dinner at one of the

local restaurants and then relaxing in the hotel room. Dusk was settling in when Brent decided to take a stroll around the hotel grounds. As with the previous night, the club across the road was vibrant and the parking lot was packed. The sound of live music percolated throughout the secluded settlement and echoed off the ravines.

He sat on a bench and was soon engrossed by the night. He grew mesmerized with the small brook that meandered along the walking trail. The background of loud music eventually succumbed to the harsh reality of racing. A podium finish was necessary in order to attract the much needed sponsorship. But despite all the diligent preparation and caution given to it, the Avenger had difficulty finishing a race.

His trance was interrupted by a soft voice beside him on the bench. "A penny for your thoughts."

It was the second time that day he was taken by surprise by that voice. "Hannah! Whoa…Hannah." He gathered his thoughts. "Where did you come from?"

"We checked in at this same hotel," she giggled. "I noticed you just sitting here all by yourself. You seemed so lost…so distant. Are you okay?"

Was her concern genuine, or some sort of diversion? He shook his head to clear his mind. "I guess I'm soothed by this babbling brook. Rocky Point is kind of tucked away out here in nowhere land." He looked around for her brother and realized they were alone. "So, where is Bro?"

Hannah slid her hands between her knees. "He's still at the track. He has to go over the kart again…for the fourteenth gazillionth time. He's such a stickler for perfection."

Brent sat on his own hands and kicked at the dirt beneath his feet. "But then, that is the making of a champion in this sport."

"Wow!" she perked. "Did I just detect a note of admiration for my brother? There just may be hope for you two boys after all."

"Hey, you're the one who said he's way too competitive."

She stiffened in her seat. "It's not all his fault. Quantum is pressuring him to enter the Kart Association Invitational at the Southern Grand Prix. They're offering him a new ride and full sponsorship. He's all beside himself." She paused for a moment. "The Invitational is part of a special Shifter Kart promotion. It'll be televised and everything. As if he isn't over-the-top gung-ho all the time anyway."

Brent should have known. His Southern GP inspiration was beginning to lose its novelty already. He searched for something to say. "Yeah, well, Harris needs to bring it down a notch." The words slipped out and he felt bad after hearing them.

Hannah's white teeth peeked through her thin lips. "Perhaps we all should."

Brent turned his face to look into her eyes. "Hey, I just meant…"

He didn't get to finish his sentence. Hannah leaned forward and brought her mouth to his. He was caught off guard. He froze. He couldn't back away. Her soft lips were moist and sweet. She moved closer and placed her hand along his cheek. His defenses were down. He had secretly wondered what kissing Hannah Branson would be like and suddenly there she was.

It was not his mother's kiss. He cupped her soft face in his hands and let himself melt.

CHAPTER 14

AS USUAL, A FEW TEAMS WERE already scattered throughout the paddock by the time Avenger Racing arrived Saturday morning. The sun had begun its ascent above the hairpin and a hearty chill hallowed the air. Empty canopies and vacated trailers added an uncanny feel to the desolate infield.

A dog barked from a couple lanes over. Subtle laughter could be heard from somewhere else. There was even a radio playing. Otherwise, the premises were quite serene.

Mac was at the side door of the trailer when he called out. "Hey, come look at this." The padlock had been forced open and then realigned to conceal the tampering.

Martin proceeded around to the back, unlocked and lowered the rear ramp. They looked in shock to see the tarps were rearranged over both karts.

"This facility is locked down and guarded at night," Mac said. "So what happened here?"

"Not what," Martin answered. "Who? Obviously someone got in here last night."

All were speechless as they assessed the situation. Brent squeezed past them and straddled the Avenger for a closer look. Then he ended the silence. "Harrison Branson!"

Martin shook his head vigorously. "Come on, Brent. Right away you make serious accusations against Harris. You have no proof of that."

Brent let their glares roll off of him. "Harris was here at the track late last night…alone."

"Now, just how would you know that?" Martin contested.

"Hannah told me," Brent divulged before thinking.

"Hannah!" Martin exclaimed. "When did Hannah tell you that? They were all still here when we left."

Brent softened his response. "We sort of crossed paths last night when I went out for my walk."

Mac frowned at Martin before turning away. Martin glared at Brent. "You and Hannah Branson went for a walk together last night?"

"No, no. Of course not," Brent quivered. "We just happened to end up on the path together." He hesitated to say anything more. "It just happened."

Mac finally chipped in on the conversation. "Well at least for now gentlemen, let's keep this to ourselves. Our relation with the Bransons right now is under scrutiny. I don't see anything in here other than somebody was snooping, but I don't want to assume things too early. Let's be alert for anything amiss."

"Yeah, well, I know it was him," Brent concluded.

"No you don't," Martin corrected. "Not for certain anyway. But I'll keep it in mind."

They rolled out the two karts and unloaded the rest

of the equipment needed for the day. Brent checked over everything that came to mind. Nothing seemed tampered with. What could have been the motive for the apparent invasion? But the bigger question was what could be the result of the invasion?

The pits were filled when the track announcer squawked the welcome message over the loud system. "Good morning racers and fans. Welcome to Rocky Point Speedway. Drivers, there is a mandatory meeting at the starting line at 7:30. Have your helmets ready for safety inspection. I repeat. That's all drivers; there is a meeting at the starting line at 7:30. We expect great weather for racing here this weekend at the Point."

The track was prepared for two full days of racing. The schedule provided equal track time for all classes. There were two-cycle, four-cycle, twin engine and shifter classes. There were classes for light weight, heavy weight, junior and senior drivers. Conveniently, Brent and Martin both were scheduled to race the same day, which meant they didn't have to stay over another night. In fact, it was already decided to make the six hour journey back home that evening.

Mac guarded the trailer during the drivers meeting. Race fans who purchased pit passes roamed the pits all morning to hang out with karts and drivers. A steady flow of curious on-lookers visited the new Avenger Racing pit. Some were very inquisitive, while others just quietly gazed from the sideline.

Martin's class was the third race, preceded by a junior four-cycle race and then a two-cycle heavy race. The first two races were both action packed crowd pleasers, bringing spectators to their feet on numerous occasions.

Martin's race did not electrify the stands the same

way. A blue Margay jumped into the lead on the first lap and ran away from the field, Avenger included. In fact, half the field finished ahead of Martin.

It was a clean race throughout, with not a single yellow flag. Even the announcer commented on the professionalism of the drivers. Avenger was mentioned only once, and that was to say it appeared to be off the pace. He went on to add the new marque that had so much promise, especially in such capable hands, did not deliver as expected.

It was not good publicity for the Avenger team. It was not the sort of reputation to inspire an influx of sponsorship.

Mac stood at trackside gritting his teeth. "Marty has to be sandbagging for some reason. Avenger is more capable than this. What is he waiting on?"

"Maybe he's just gun shy of another DNF," Brent reasoned.

"That's not your uncle," Mac argued. "He ran better than this in practice yesterday. Something isn't right."

At the checkered flag, Avenger was in eighth place, mid pack, and definitely out of trophy range. It coasted to the weight scales having finished its first race under its own power. Even so, Martin was visibly disappointed.

"I had plenty of power off the corners," he explained. "But top-end just dropped off. I was down a good 800 rpms if not more." He tossed his helmet on the seat. "Now its carburetion."

"No way," Mac complained. "That carb is right on." He bent down to examine the throttle linkage. He pulled a flat screwdriver from his back pocket, removed the air filter and looked straight into the bore of the carb.

"You're right, Marty, top-end is off." He worked the throttle cable open and closed. "The butterfly is opening so far that it's starting to close again. You weren't running full throttle."

Martin shook his head. "That throttle stop was adjusted when I built that carb."

Mac stood up and flipped the screwdriver in his hand several times. "That was before the break-in last night. Something bent the stop so the throttle starts to close again."

"Something?" Brent questioned. "Or someone?"

They exchanged grave looks. Martin's jaw tightened. "Snooping is one thing. But I really hate to think that someone intentionally sabotaged our karts last night."

Mac already had the air filter off of the sprinter. "I could accept an error on your part with one carb, but this stop is bent the same way."

Obviously, Brent's kart was also affected and his performance would be compromised accordingly. "That Branson jerk crossed the line this time," he snapped, spinning toward pit road. "I'm gonna…"

Martin grabbed his nephew. "Brent, we don't know that for sure and we'll not make any accusations until we do. You can't go after someone half cocked like that."

"Watch me!"

"No, Brent," Mac declared. "You know Marty's right. We'll get to the bottom of this, but not until we know for sure who it is. You're one strike away from getting us black-balled. Luckily, we caught this before your race. It's an easy fix. Add this to our pre-check list from now on."

As individual battles raged out on the track in the

fourth race, Brent struggled with an inward battle of his own. To lose to an opponent fair and square on the race track was tough enough. But to be cheated off track by some lowly act of sabotage could never be tolerated. Martin was cheated. The Avenger name was being dishonored and Brent would have to redeem the namesake.

"Now you really have to stay out of my way, Branson…sister or no sister," Brent said under his breath. He grappled with the thought that Hannah may have been part of such an act; that she could have just been a convenient distraction. After last night, he was more confused than ever.

CHAPTER 15

FOR THE SECLUDED, MOUNTAINOUS establishment that Rocky Point was, the speedway drew an effervescent crowd. Despite having no residential district to support the area, the racing events pulled in a fan base from all along the interstate. By the time of Brent's mid-afternoon race, spectators not only filled the modest grandstand, but they had the fence area jam-packed from one end of the front straightaway to the other. Obviously that hide-away speedway was the entertainment venue for the entire region.

Mixed with the scent of racing fuel and exhaust fumes was the hovering aroma of grilled burgers, French fries and hot dogs.

Mac adjusted the throttle stop while Brent double-checked for any other possible deficiency. Martin struggled to get beyond the poor showing in his own race. "Let this be a lesson. We have to be conscientious with our preparations. Leave no assumptions."

Brent responded at the first call to the pre-grid

halfway through the preceding race. One of the first to arrive, he placed the Avenger in its assigned spot in 11th position and rested on the pit wall to watch his competitors file in.

Eventually the Bransons showed up and took their places halfway up the line. Hannah smiled and waved even as her brother engaged her in some sort of animated directive, waving his arms and deferring her attention to their karts. Brent couldn't return the wave. His jaw hardened at the mere thought that Harris may have been responsible for last night's intrusion. Considering the personality differences between those siblings, it was hard to imagine they could even be related. He peered at them resentfully.

Martin arrived with the electric starter and read Brent's contemplation. "You're eating yourself up over Harrison Branson," he warned. "He isn't worth it. Just clear him out of your mind. This situation will not get fixed out there on the race track."

"It might help though if we knock his ego down a notch out there."

"No, Brent," Martin ordered. "Just let it go!"

"Uncle Martin, if he thought I did something like that to him, he'd have me in front of the officials in a heartbeat."

Martin slumped beside him on the wall. "Perhaps, but first he'd have to prove it. And secondly, you wouldn't do it in the first place."

"But that wouldn't stop…"

"I said let it go!"

Karts blipped and popped into the pits as they came off the course following their cool down lap. Brent reached for his helmet. "Okay, I let it go!" But he knew he couldn't. And from the way Martin was eyeing him, he knew he hadn't convinced him either.

The usual butterflies in Brent's stomach waiting for the green flag to drop were gone. Maybe it was his eagerness to cut loose. Maybe it was his confidence with the course. Whatever it was, it made his focus intense.

The swirl of green!

The Avenger burst onto the track and shot immediately to the other side. It blasted past a throng of karts mingled together still trying to clear the grid. One of those confined in the bedlam was Harrison Branson.

Too easy, Brent thought. He slipped past two more karts without a hint of hesitation. By the elevated backstretch, he had piloted his way into second place. He found it ironic that it was Colton who was leading.

Brent chuckled. *There is such a chase for funding, yet it's a used nickel and dime contraption that gets the job done. Boy, never judge a book by its cover.*

As he dove into Turn 11 to launch wide onto the main straight, he glance across his shoulder to check on his pursuers. All he could see was one tightly bunched horde coming around the embankment that hid Turn 10.

The Avenger never overtook the race leader, but stayed glued to its push bar for the entire race. Although the kart looked questionable, Colton himself demonstrated true championship form. He drove a very tight, calculated race. His late apex on every turn was an unusual line. But his technique was foolproof. He possessed the experience and apparently the equipment to get the job done.

Colton finished first, with the Avenger in tow for a solid, unchallenged second. Together they lapped half of the field. Both Bransons finished somewhere mid-pack, never once in contention. In fact, they were in the cross hairs to also be lapped by the lead duo.

The PA system commended the Avenger during the cool down lap. "The controversial Avenger kart finally demonstrated its prowess here today, folks. Brent Lockeman apparently overcame the gremlins that haunted the new racing team earlier."

When Brent killed the motor in the weight scale line, Martin was waiting there to embrace him. "Good job! You pulled us out of the basement with that one. Avenger Racing got great coverage the whole time."

But the elation was short-lived. Leading a group of spirited followers, Harris Branson stormed them with his fists waving in the air.

"You crossed the line this time, Lockeman," he shouted. "I won't stand to be sabotaged. You're going down!"

Before his advances reached Brent, Mac ambushed the raging assailant in a bear hug. Brent reacted in self-defense with clenched fists as Martin seized his nephew and pulled him away. The stirred crowd cheered in support of the pending brawl.

Track officials jumped into the midst of the turmoil. "Both of you to registration!" yelled the official with 'Race Director' on his white shirt. "Now!" He reached for Harrison's collar but Harris shook off the grasp.

"This punk vandalized my kart," Harris screamed at the director. "I demand..."

"That is bull!" Brent shouted, lurching toward him. A second official stepped in to intervene.

"To registration!" the race director ordered again. "We will not tolerate this sort of behavior. I'm well aware that you boys had some personal issues before. We will deal with this in the registration office." His stern demeanor rang with authority.

Martin relaxed his hold on Brent. "Now just may be the time to hash this out after all. I have something to say in all of this too. Let's take this before the stewards."

"That's fine with me!" Harris snapped as Mac released him. He shuffled his arms loose in defiance. "You're through, Lockeman." He abruptly spun and marched toward registration. "We'll put an end to your shenanigans."

As Brent stepped out into the crowd, he noticed Hannah just beyond them in the distance. Exhibiting no emotion one way or another, she turned and headed in the opposite direction toward her pit and left her kart in the scale line.

A parade followed the walk down pit road. Karts lining up for the next race were abandoned as people left the grid to get in on the commotion. The PA system ordered everyone back to their places in order to get the race underway. Fortunately, tempers had a chance to cool off along the way.

The race director closed the door to the meeting room for privacy. He turned his attention to Martin first. "Mr. Kessick, let me just start by saying although we never met, I have a lot of respect for you and your previous racing accomplishments. So, what is the something you have to say in all of this?"

Martin cleared his throat. "Thank you. First of all what we have here is a pair of highly motivated and perhaps overly strong-willed competitors. That's not necessarily a bad thing as long as we get a handle on it."

The director cut in. "Oh, believe me Mr. Kessick, we're going to do just that...right now."

Martin raised his hands in surrender mode. "Let me just say something about this weekend. We have been accused of vandalism when in fact our trailer was broken into sometime last night. Our carburetors were tampered with in an attempt to compromise our performance today."

Harris puffed. "Your kart seemed to be working just fine today. It was mine that was screwed with."

"Correction there, Harrison," Martin argued. "My enduro somehow had an altered throttle stop. But we fixed it on the sprinter before Brent's race or he would have suffered as well."

Harris countered angrily. "Are you saying you had nothing to do with our ruin today? My sister's kart suffered too."

"Are you saying you had nothing to do with our break-in last night?" Brent retorted. "You were here after hours. You had motive and opportunity."

"There were at least a dozen others here after hours last night," Harris blurted. "I win fair and square. I surely don't have to cheat to whip you."

"We would never stoop to jinx a competitor's equipment," Martin said. "Avenger Racing is straight up."

"Well, obviously somebody did," Harris charged.

The race director waved his hands to cut in. "It seems we have some misguided perceptions here, gentlemen. Apparently someone out there wants both of you off the podium, and you think it's each other." There was a pause as he considered the next course of action. "What I'm hearing is serious. I wasn't expecting anything like this. I believe the Board has a situation to consider at the next meeting and I will see to it that it gets addressed. But as for the present, we cannot allow fighting at our events."

Martin agreed. "You're absolutely right, Sir. But technically there was no fight, only a heated argument, and one of apparent misunderstanding at that. Luckily we intercepted in time."

The director frowned and looked at the two co-officials in the room. They both shrugged.

"Okay," the boss said. "I'll play along...this time. But this incident goes in my report along with the notion that we have a vandal among us." He gave a stern look at Brent and Harris. "You are both on notice...if I even smell something brewing between you boys again; I will have you suspended from the series for the rest of the season. Is that clear?"

"Yes."

"Yes sir"

He shook his head. "Good. Now stay away from each other."

Harris threw a sideways glance to Brent. "And you stay away from my sister. She doesn't like you. She just feels sorry for you."

Brent's jaw tightened at the insinuation. "That's not for you to decide."

Harris pointed at him piercingly. "I am deciding. Stay away from her!"

"Only when she tells me that...not you!"

The director interrupted. "Boys, boys. This isn't smelling good to me. Remember, don't make me be the bad guy here."

Martin grabbed Brent's shoulder and steered him toward the door. "Thank you, Sir."

"Don't thank me yet, Mr. Kessick. It seems to me you have a huge task on your hands."

CHAPTER 16

KATHERINE SAT ALONE AT THE kitchen table with both hands cupped around a hot, steamy coffee. She seemed lost in thought as she stared through the window across the room at a peaceful pink sunrise painted on the horizon.

"Morning, Mom," Brent muttered as he placed a dry bowl of cereal beside her along with a carton of milk to dowse on it. He slumped into a chair and wiped his drowsy eyes. "We got in late last night from Rocky Point and I didn't want to disturb you."

Katherine continued to stare out the window.

Brent poured milk on the cereal. "We made a decent showing, not quite as grand as we had hoped for, but decent."

Katherine's gaze dropped to her cup of coffee. "Honey, it's time you and I had a talk."

Brent grimaced. "Mom, look. I know you don't approve of my racing. We've had that talk. I want you to understand…"

She leveled her head to face him. "For once, you have to listen to what I'm about to say, Brent."

"Mom," he huffed. "Uncle Martin and I have assured you…"

"Stop, Brent!" she snapped, "and listen to me. What I'm about to say is not about you and Marty. This is not about the Avenger or your obsession to go racing. I need to discuss something very serious with you, something about me."

Brent sat back into the chair and looked into her moist eyes. A tear trickled over her cheek and along side her nose. This was serious. Silence prevailed. He swallowed a lump that formed in his throat. "Mom, what's wrong? What is it?"

She gazed back down into her cup of coffee that was no longer steaming. "I have to share something with you. Promise me you will hear me out before you jump to conclusions. Take as long as you like before you respond."

Brent exhaled a slow stream of air, a calming breath, a cleansing breath. He realized how his mother could be overly emotional at times, but her tears were convicting. "Mom, what's wrong?" he repeated.

The side of her mouth twitched. "Wrong? I'm not saying anything is wrong. I suppose we'll decipher that later." She took a sip of her cold coffee. "Bobby asked me to marry him."

Brent slumped. His head bowed and his shoulders drooped. His arms fell to his lap. "Wow! Nothing like breaking it to me easy there, Mom. That was a blow!"

"I said to take your time with this," she reminded him. "I said to hear me out first."

"What is there to hear out? I'd say you pretty much got it all out in one gulp."

She tried for a comforting smile. "I guess the only way to say this is to be straight and direct. You had to expect it was coming sometime."

"No," Brent admitted. "I didn't. He's been sweet on you, yes. He's been wiggling his way in, yes. I just never thought you'd let it get this far."

"You mean you hoped it wouldn't. But did you ever think that just maybe I care a little bit about him too."

"A little bit?" Brent scoffed. "Mom, you're talking marriage here. The guy is a jerk!"

"Brent!" she snapped. "I asked you before not to speak about Bobby like that. Now I'm telling you. You will not refer to Robert Wheeling as a jerk...ever again and that is an order. I won't stand for it! He is a very dear and close friend...and he has been for some time now. I am not jumping into this blindly, believe me. It's time you get beyond your dislike for him and give him a chance. Get to know the man. You will like him."

"Is that an order too?"

"I didn't mean for it to come out that way, Honey. That was callous of me. I apologize. But enough is enough. It's time you be fair about this."

Brent stared at his milky cereal. "It sounds like your mind is already made up. You accepted his proposal didn't you?"

"For your information," she murmured, "I still consider your feelings in the matter, even though I don't think you're being fair. Honey, it's been three years now since your father passed away. I grieve everyday for him just as I know you do. But, Brent, I didn't die that day, and neither did you. We both have to move on with our future. And it will only be what we make it. When will you realize that?"

"I'm working on that future, Mom. Uncle Martin is part of that future for us."

"For us? Honey, racing is not my future. And I'm still not convinced that it's yours either. I have to come to terms with the fact that you are growing up and you have to start making your own decisions. But I have to make decisions for myself too. I can't live in a vacuum the rest of my life."

"How do you know Wheeling isn't a vacuum? Who else have you even dated?"

Katherine looked intently at her son. "And who else would you have approved of had I gone out with others? I don't have to play the field to find Mr. Right. I think by now I have enough foresight to know."

Brent chomped on a scoop of soggy, tasteless cereal. Though reluctant to admit it, he knew everything she said was right. He knew in his heart she was right. He respected her for that. So why was he contesting her now?

He chomped on another scoop of cereal as one last rush of reasoning ventured through his mind. "Bob Wheeling is an egotistical, arrogant salesman. I just don't want you being his latest conquest."

Katherine propped her chin on her palms. "Egotistical, arrogant salesman? It sounds like you just called him a jerk but in a different way."

Brent had to grin. "I have my orders."

His mother smiled for the first time. "You always had a knack of putting your own spin on things. You take after your father in that." She stroked his fluffy hair. "You just might pull off this racing dream of yours yet."

Brent frowned. "This dream will quickly become a nightmare if we don't secure some sort of sponsorship soon."

Katherine acknowledged. "Suz told me Mac and Marty are feeling the pinch of financing in this down economy. Mac's hardware business is holding its own but there is no excess. And we know all about the recession Marty's construction business is in. That's why he took on those small commercial jobs. It's tough right now for him and Suz. But you said you had a good showing this weekend. That's what you needed, right?"

Brent ate the last of his cereal. "I took a second. Uncle Martin didn't place. The announcer gave us some bad publicity. How do you lure financial support if you don't have results? Nobody wants to back a loser."

"Brent, you have to let Mac and Marty handle that. They have the business sense for it. Trust me. If it's meant to be, then they'll work it out."

Brent nodded. "Yeah, well, along with all of that, someone is purposely out to jinx us. The trailer was broken into Friday night and someone meddled with our carbs. We caught it in time for my race, but it cost Uncle Martin his."

"My gosh! This is getting serious. I had no idea. What are you going to do?"

"Well, I thought I knew who it was, but now I'm not so sure. The race officials are aware of it so hopefully it won't happen again."

Her face showed concern. "Does it have anything to do with that angry boy in the purple and yellow kart? You know, the one that gave you all that trouble at Conleyville?"

"We're not sure. The Bransons may have been a target also. It appears the same thing happened to them."

"You stay away from those people. They seem like bad news. Is that the girl you're getting soft about?"

Suddenly, Brent's senses went on high alert. He

was flooded with caution. How could his mother possibly come to such a conclusion about Hannah Branson? Has something become too obvious? He never confirmed anything about Hannah to anyone, had he? "Mom, where is this coming from?"

She had the look on her face called mother's intuition. Brent recognized that look many times growing up. It was the very look that suggested she was always on to him. "Your friend Kimmie mentioned her from time to time. And your Aunt Suz can spot that sort of thing."

"Spot what sort of thing?" Brent asked.

"Brent, come on. You're not a child anymore. You will develop relationships. I can see these things too. Give me credit for being a mother."

"Oh, who's talking about relationships?"

She chuckled. "So then it's true?"

"No!" he barked. "I mean, what are you implying? There is no relationship." He felt himself blush. "You never answered me about whether you accepted Wheeling's proposal."

Katherine threw her hands in the air. "You just did it again. You just put a spin on our discussion."

It was Brent's turn to chuckle. "You said to take as much time as I need to respond. Okay, it looks like we both need to take some time."

She frowned. "Sometimes you can be so mature about things. It's hard for me to come to terms with the fact that you really are growing up. And it scares me."

CHAPTER 17

ON MONDAY MORNING, THE L&M Hardware business was proof that even in sluggish times the shop work can get backed up if someone isn't there to service the orders that filter in. While chasing the enduro circuit, Mac's service area filled up with mower blades to be sharpened, small engines to be tuned and other routine maintenance issues. All of which was great for Mac and his business.

Since Martin was getting caught up on his small construction contracts, he was able to assist with the shop's latest spurt in workload.

There wasn't much they could do with the Avenger since they depleted the supply of components. Their original plan to assemble an extra kart for reserve was put on hold until they secured funding. Composite bodies for another sprint and enduro sat along the back wall but the other parts were needed to complete them.

Brent rebuilt a finicky chainsaw carburetor that had to go out that day, and then spent the rest of the morning sharpening mower blades. Mac spent the morning on a major welding repair on a lawn tractor he insisted should be melted down and recycled. Martin assembled and prepped a new mower a customer was waiting to pick up.

Morale in the shop was high concerning the hardware business. However the mood was gloomy concerning Avenger Racing. If the new marque was to survive it needed a prescriptive shot-in-the-arm. And for the racing world to take it seriously, it had to take itself seriously.

Brent believed in Avenger Racing and deep down he felt his uncle did also. But he began to realize the complexity of the challenges they faced in getting it taken seriously.

Martin chomped on a ham and cheese sandwich during the break for lunch. "Mac, Brent and I will cover you here. I think you have to convert those two bodies back there on the shelf into rollers to have for display on the circuit. We have to convince the racing community that Avenger Racing is open for business."

"We haven't been real convincing with our record so far," Mac stated nonchalantly. "We need a big break."

Brent couldn't resist the pitch. "The Southern Grand Prix will give us that. It will be great exposure to the sports car racers, too. As part of the shifter kart promotion, they're planning a full media bliss, including televised coverage."

"Televised?" Martin asked. "Where did you get that from?"

"I heard about it," Brent answered, though he stopped short of further explanation.

"Wow!" Martin took another bite from his sandwich. "This is sounding better and better by the minute."

Mac perked up. "Then we have to step up our game...big time. No more embarrassing, two bit part failures or unexpected saboteurs. We need a load of spares, including a variety of tire compounds. We have to be ready for whatever Heartland Motor Speedway throws at us."

Brent perked with excitement. "Can we hit up Malta Tire for support again like we did at the Silva race two years ago? We have back-up motors if we need them. And why do we really need spare karts?"

Martin shrugged. "The two rollers will at least help generate good media exposure. I'll call Wil Sowers at Malta and hype the Grand Prix. The SCCA presence would be a great marketing strategy for him."

Elation overwhelmed the earlier gloom.

"So then," Brent reasoned. "Can we do this?"

Mac formed half a grin in agreement. "But like I said earlier, we have to step up our game. This is last minute, crunch time stuff. But, yes, I believe we can do it."

Martin half-grinned also. "I never ran Heartland before. But I hear it's a well-groomed, highly manicured, country club establishment. A fine facility...two and a half miles of beautiful rural farmland."

Mac joked. "You talk as if you plan to farm on it instead of race on it."

"Hey!" Martin chuckled. "If Avenger Racing can pull this off it may well be farming. We'll be planting a seed there to see how it grows."

Brent qualified his earlier statement. "So then, we can do this!"

There was a round of high fives among them.

"I guess we'll give it a shot," Martin quipped.

Brent exploded with enthusiasm. "Yeah!" he

squealed.

"Let's get cracking then," Mac added.

Brent looked at the two molded bodies on the back shelf and envisioned them rolling off the trailer at the race track. Down on finances, but up on commitment, that was Avenger Racing. It was alive.

The pep rally boosted morale for the rest of the day. The smell of hope finally lingered in the air, if only imagined. Brent finished sharpening the stack of mower blades with a song in his heart.

When he returned home with Martin that evening, Robert Wheeling's SUV was just pulling out of the driveway. So went the song in Brent's heart.

"Hi, Sweetie," Katherine called out from the living room. "I'm glad you're home. I want to talk to you about something if you have a moment."

Brent reached the top of the stairway. *Uh oh*, he thought to himself. These talks have not gone the best lately. "Sure, Mom. What's up?"

She motioned toward the sofa. "Sit down."

Uh oh, he thought again. *Strike two coming up.* He lowered himself onto the sofa skeptically.

She exhaled a cleansing breath before speaking. "Bobby wants to talk to you about us. He wants to explain his feelings for me and ask you in person for your approval to marry me. He respects you enough to want you involved in the matter."

"He was sure to run out of here quick enough as soon as I got home."

"He had to leave for a showing at one of his properties." She considered how to proceed next. "I suggested it would be better if I talked with you first. I know how you feel about him and I want to avoid a confrontation."

Brent shook his head. "Mom, we already had this discussion. It is your decision to marry him, not mine."

"No," she insisted. "It is our decision, and I told him that. You are the main aspect of my life."

"What if he and I can't get along, Mom? You would be caught in the middle. I don't want that."

Katherine raised her hands. "Brent, I just know once you give him a chance, it will work out. I know you. And I know Bobby. I would never consider this proposal if I thought there would be a problem."

Brent sat quietly pondering what to say.

She continued before he got the chance. "Robert is really a very nice man, one who can provide for us. He wants to be part of our lives Honey, and he wants us to be part of his."

He felt the sincerity in his mother's heart. Perhaps he had rushed to his judgment of Robert Wheeling, the Realtor, the entrepreneur, the fancy dresser and talker. After all, how well did he really know the man? Maybe time would provide for a better relationship between them as she often suggested. Surely he could trust his mother's intuition in the matter. Could he give it the chance it deserved before casting it all aside prematurely?

He rose from the sofa. "What do I call him?"

Katherine brushed a strand of hair away from her face. "He's not your father. His name is Robert. You can call him Bobby."

"Then tell him my name is Brent. I don't like his 'my boy' inference."

"You should tell him that when the two of you talk. It could be one of those foundational things between you."

Brent smirked. "It may only be the start of many foundational things."

128

"It may indeed," Katherine smiled. "See there, I knew we could work this out."

CHAPTER 18

THE INSPIRATION OF THE UPCOMING Southern Grand Prix boosted the mood in the Avenger shop all week long. Mac assembled the pair of spare bodies into rolling chassis with the remaining components he had on hand. Martin blueprinted a pair of new Yamaha KT 100 motors he had ordered on credit earlier, while Brent rebuilt the last two axle clutches they had on the shelf.

"This is what you call optimization of inventory," Martin commented jokingly, but with a serious implication.

Late on Wednesday afternoon, Martin's tire rep from Malta, Wilbur Sowers, visited the shop. Though only middle-aged, his gray hair was beyond his years. Brent thought in the past it might actually be highlighted that way. It wasn't. It was a simple, pre-mature gray.

Wilbur was a tall, boisterous speaking man. "Marty, I haven't heard from you guys in ages," he said, strutting across the shop. "I'm glad to see you're jumping back onto the racing scene again. I heard some rumors about Kessick's new Avenger, but nothing solid."

Martin shook his old acquaintance's hand. "Maybe that's because we're still struggling to make it solid. Surely of all people, you know the rigors of product development."

"Yes, yes indeed," Wil stated animatedly. "That tire model you helped me launch at the Silva Endurance race two years ago really took off for us. We developed a directional tire in that series which is performing well at Indy and in the Formula One ranks."

"Great!" Martin exclaimed. "I'm glad we could help, which brings me to this, Wil. We need a supply of road racing tires for the Southern GP. You know I hate to pitch it to you this way, but with the current state of the economy, the funds are down. What are the chances for Malta Tire to sponsor us?"

"Marty, you know better than to feel guilty about pitching to Malta. In fact, we recently cast some kart tires with a different wear compound. Since they're so simple to test production with, I have a couple left over from the initial run. I'll put a package together for you."

"Thank you," Mac said. "Has any testing been done on them yet?"

Wilbur shrugged. "Actually, we're straightening out an issue right now with a new oriented strand core we developed. We're trying the different wear compound as a fix...so no...not yet. That's the hiccup that comes along with research and development. But we're sponsoring a sports car team that's going to the Southern and we're confident we have improved it. As far as testing goes, I'm looking forward to the results I know I can get from you guys."

"Count us in then," Martin said. "We're running both the new sit-up and lay-down chassis so we have no performance data from the Heartland Speedway to supply you with."

"Marty, Marty, Marty," Wil quipped. "You're talking to your old buddy Wil here. I know how you guys run and I have data from our sports car people on the Heartland facility. I'll have you ready to go from my end. You just be ready to go from yours."

Wilbur spent the rest of his visit viewing the shop and checking out the new reinforced composite Avengers. Though impressed with what he saw, he was clearly not a chassis engineer. He was a tire man, proficient in the curing and heat cycling of rubber compounds, tire grip and wear. But as far as Brent was concerned, that was sufficient. A good tire man on any racing team is priceless.

They worked as best they could with the components they had to finish the two racing Avengers plus the two rollers. Mac had previously fabricated just enough new spindles for each kart. When they were finished they had no more axles, brakes, fuel tanks or steering parts left. Brent wasn't sure what they would do next, but neither Mac nor Martin seemed to let it bother them. If they had further concerns, they concealed it well. There was a sense of 'run till you're done' frame of mind.

Bobby Wheeling came to the house again on Saturday evening to take Katherine out for a late dinner. Brent found himself in the unwanted position of sitting with him in the living room, waiting as his mother got herself ready. The thought even crossed his mind perhaps it was planned that way.

"Well, Brent, my boy," Bobby broke the icy silence. "Katherine has informed me you have accepted our plans to marry. I'm glad. We wanted your blessing. Your acceptance means a lot to both of us. I'm extremely fond of your mother and I look forward to having her by my side for the rest of my life."

Brent was still inwardly gagging over the 'my boy' reference when he heard the last line. "So…you could have just offered her a partnership in your firm."

Bobby's face went blank as he absently adjusted the lapel on his sport coat, even though it wasn't needed.

Brent broke the heaviness with a thin smile. "I'm sorry, Mr. Wheeling. That was one of those things that just popped out of my mouth. It's out of my system now." He paused. "I want you to know I wish the best for the two of you. You do have my approval."

Bobby looked at the floor before looking up with a thin smile of his own. "I must tell you I really do appreciate your candidness. Actually, I admire that. I trust I will always have your honesty. It will help me to understand you better as we go forward…and I think I do already." He extended his right hand in friendship.

Oh no, Brent thought to himself. *It's always like a business transaction with this guy.* He shook the hand nevertheless. "Congratulations."

Katherine called from the bedroom. "I'll be out in a minute, boys. Get acquainted awhile."

They shared a laugh for the first time.

"So, how's the racing going, my boy?" Bobby asked genuinely.

Brent couldn't squelch the urge any longer. "You have to cut it with the 'my boy' stuff, Mr. Wheeling. Could you please just call me Brent?"

"Okay, if you'll not call me Mr. Wheeling any longer. It's far too formal. Call me Bobby."

Suddenly Brent felt more relaxed. "Fair enough." He returned to the original question. "We're taking a break from the Enduro circuit right now to make a run in the Southern Grand Prix. We hope for some good media coverage from the Karting Invitational there. With the right backing and of course the right luck, it could be Avenger Racing's big debut."

"I'd like to join you at the track sometime," Bobby said. "It sounds like fun. Katherine speaks highly of you and Marty's accomplishments."

"Sure. Bring Mom out to the races sometime. I've been trying to get her more comfortable with the idea since, well, forever."

"I'll do that," Bobby replied. "It'll be a nice break from some stuffy real estate deals all the time."

Katherine emerged from the bedroom looking stunning. She wore a snug fitting pants suit and vest with her hair teasingly tossed to one side. "How are my boys doing out here?"

Brent and Bobby looked at her, neither one able to answer her question. Then they looked at each other, waiting to see which one would be the first to speak.

It was Brent. "Wow, Mom! I don't think I can allow you to go out looking like that. What would people think?"

Bobby bounced to his feet. "Let me handle that, my boy."

Katherine caught the 'my boy' inference again and shot a serious glance toward Brent.

Bobby caught it at the same time. "I'm sorry, Brent. That was just one of those things that popped out of my mouth. I think it's out of my system now." He said it with sincerity.

Katherine threw a puzzled look as the two men laughed.

Bobby took her gently by the arm. "What I meant to say, Brent, is that I will gladly be your mother's noble defender tonight." He turned to her directly. "Shall we venture into thy kingdom, my Lady?"

She smiled from ear to ear. "Oh, why indeed, my honorable Sir."

Brent waved his hand farewell as he slumped into the cushion of the sofa. It was becoming almost too playful.

"Go!" he halfheartedly played along. "Thy peasant boy shall fend for thyself 'tis night, my fair maiden."

CHAPTER 19

SEVERAL ISSUES WERE RESOLVED the following week as they prepared for that weekend's Southern Grand Prix. Registration for the pair of Avengers was confirmed as well as reservations and other travel arrangements.

Martin had an emergency roof tear-off and replacement which occupied his work days. So Mac finished the carburetor work for him and tuned the new motors on the shop's dyno. They were all pleased with the numbers the testing provided.

Brent maintained the customer service orders that always seemed to increase during the week of an upcoming major race. The anxiety he felt though was more than usual. There was more at stake than merely finishing the karts. Everything they did, they checked twice. Steering and brake hardware, throttle adjustments and torque settings were rechecked. The paranoia of neglect was overwhelming.

On Wednesday evening, Martin stopped by the shop to pick up Brent on his way home as usual. "Mac, do you remember Jerry Stiles from Stiles Exhausts?"

Mac chuckled. "Sure! Now there's a name from the past for ya. I can't tell you when I heard from those guys last. Are they still pushing that pipe-of-the-month thing? Do you remember how they kept hitting the market with some latest-and-greatest exhaust system every other month? It got hard to keep up with."

Martin nodded. "Yeah, that was tough alright. Well, anyway, I spoke with Jerry on the phone today. They are into making headers for drag racers now. But he told me he had a little product on the back burner about a year ago…a new two-cycle can, that got sidetracked due to a drag header project."

Mac laid down his socket wrench. "What about it?"

"He called it the Z2 because of a revolutionary two-zone baffle he designed. He said it tested very well on their dyno."

Mac's eyebrow lifted. "And you're about to tell me he has a couple lying around we can try out now, right?"

Martin laughed. "Just the prototype. But he was excited to loan it to us for the Grand Prix. I asked if he could scrounge up an extra one for us." He shrugged and then grinned. "He said he'll have it to me this week yet."

Brent was puzzled. "So what does a Z2 mean for us?"

Mac retrieved his socket wrench. "It means we'll be re-tuning those motors I just spent all that dyno time on."

"Why?" Brent asked. "You have them setup and ready to go."

Martin shook his head. "It's optimum tuning. A pipe is designed for a particular flow. Different flow designs peak at different power ranges. We have to tune our motors to the new Z2 pipe, whatever it calls for. Exhaust tuning is crucial on a 2-cycle engine."

Brent rested against the workbench in deep thought. "So, let me see if I have this straight. We are going into a big race, at an unfamiliar track, with an untested tire and an unproven exhaust system. And all of that is in addition to a kart still trying to establish itself with a race team that is overstretched and under-funded. Do I have that right?"

Mac tried to mask his amusement. "And what's your point?"

"My point!" Brent blurted. "My point is what security is that supposed to give me. I mean, come on fellas. I could use a little confidence boost here."

"Confidence," Martin explained, "has to be in you. If you don't believe in yourself, then no one else will either. Innovation is nothing until it is proven. Let's face it, some ideas fail. In fact, more ideas fail than succeed. But when an idea works, it sets the new standard. In the 1960's, a certain plastic car with an automatic transmission, Chevy engine and movable airplane wings met with its share of critics. But Texas oilman Jim Hall's Chaparrals silenced all the nay-sayers. The confidence in himself and his ideas was all he needed."

"Stated like a true champion," Mac praised. "Marty, you should write a motivational book."

"Maybe I will…if we pull this off," Martin boasted.

Mac laughed. "What do you mean, if we pull this off? Where is that confidence you just jabbered about?"

Martin was already laughing with him. "Confidence? The Avenger is unreliable, our tires are unconfirmed and we have no idea how some new two-stage exhaust pipe will work out. Confidence?" he repeated.

"Okay, okay. I get it guys," Brent surrendered. "Excuse me for being the realist here."

When Brent returned home later, Katherine was sitting alone at the kitchen table as if she was waiting for him again. "Another long day, Honey?" she asked in her soft yet concerning voice. But somehow it didn't seem like a question. "You are wearing yourself out over this racing thing. You can't keep going on like this."

Brent dropped onto the chair across from her. "It's only until the Grand Prix. Then things will be back to normal."

"Will things ever be back to normal?" She sipped from her cup of coffee. "There will always be the next big race, the next big commitment. Brent, don't you know this is only the beginning of it all?"

"Mom, I have to do this."

"This what? This racing? You and Marty started this as a fun little hobby two years ago and now look at you guys…building cars and motors and Grand Prix racing. And that's another thing. When were you going to tell me about this Grand Prix thing? I had to hear about it from Bobby. You need to confide in me with these things, Brent. I don't know if you're coming or going anymore."

"Mom, I told you before, this is what I want. I have a chance right now to go for it and I have to take it. Too many people live a life they don't want because they never go for the life they do want."

She reached across the table and placed her hand on his. "Honey, how can you even think you know what you want in life yet? Don't get so caught up in today that you lose sight of tomorrow. You're trying to grow up too fast. You're taking everything too fast. I watch you on that race track and it scares me. Those other people scare me. Slow your life down once, Brent, before it crashes down around you."

"Mom, what are you talking about? I am 15 years old. I do know what I want. I want to be part of Avenger Racing. I've learned so much these past two years from Uncle Martin I can't begin to explain to you. And there is so much more to learn." He studied her worried face. "I've never been so charged about anything in my life."

She squeezed his hand firmly. "That's what worries me...that you're so charged up. And Marty is struggling with this more than he'll let on to you. You guys have to slow this down before it's too late."

"Too late for what?"

"Too late to recover from the financial burden, Brent. Suz told me Marty is becoming obsessed with this. He is pouring everything he has, everything they have, into this. She's as concerned as am I." She hung her head and was silent for a moment. "You dug out Marty's old kart two years ago and got him racing again. You convinced him to go to that big Silva race. Now he has the fever to start his own kart racing company. And you have him all psyched into this Grand Prix. Brent, when will you stop?"

Why did her words always drown his soul? How bad was it for Uncle Martin and Aunt Suz? Have they sheltered Brent from an agony they concealed? To campaign in the Southern Grand Prix with the Avenger would be the ultimate experience. But what if disaster struck again; another episode of sabotage or another failed outcome? Could they afford a wasted investment in a flimsy dream? Had Brent let himself be part of a ruin that awaited them? Was he to be their financial demise? He really had no idea all that was at stake.

He rose from his chair. "Mom, pray for us then. Something is already in motion. Just pray it's the right something."

CHAPTER 20

IT WAS A TWELVE HOUR DRIVE TO Heartland Motor Speedway. Road trips and hotels were part of the National circuit, as well as dedication, a dedication of both time and money. Avenger Racing couldn't be more blessed with the deep rooted dedication of time, but the money part was more severe.

The drive was a quiet twelve hours, hopeful, positive and encouraging...but quiet. As the miles rolled beneath their wheels, all three men pondered the same thoughts, only no one voiced them.

Riding along mesmerized, staring through the glass as the countryside passed by, Brent welcomed the chance to prove the merits of Avenger Racing. Yet he could not brush away the concern he had of the real cost to those deeply connected. Mac's sacrifice was evident by his unrelenting donation of time and resources toward the Avenger's development. And his mother's words that Uncle Martin and Aunt Suz had everything on the line haunted him. He understood the value that came from the support of having such partners as Stiles Exhaust and

Malta Tires. But he also understood there had to be more. Something else was needed to pay the bills. He shouldered the burden that his contribution was to prove it was all worth it...and to win!

They rolled through the speedway gate late Thursday night an hour and a half before it closed for the day. Some race teams were already there while others would arrive Friday. Those who show up in between would wait in a line along the fence until the gates reopened at 6 o'clock in the morning.

Brent was satisfied to get there in time to select a good pit space and get a decent night's sleep. They would camp on the premises in the trailer for the weekend. The infield showers and restroom facilities were updated and clean, and the night air was refreshing. After a day on the road the air mattress was a welcomed relief.

Brent was awakened the next morning to the disconcerting idle of incoming trucks and trailers. Mac and Martin were up and had the canopy erected. The two Avenger rollers were already out on display in front of the trailer for the world to see.

"We want to be on the track when practice opens at 9 o'clock," Martin announced. "Safety tech opens at 8 over by the weight scales."

Brent wiped the sleep from his eyes. "Why didn't you wake me to help set up?"

Mac sipped a fresh brewed coffee. "You need your sleep. We have this covered."

Some sports cars were on the track for practice as Brent waited in line with his kart for tech to open. At the front of the line was none other than the Colton brothers. Brent nodded a pleasant welcome but the pair intentionally looked the other way. Brent shook his head. They were without a doubt a strange breed.

You guys are so arrogant you apparently don't need money, he thought. *But yet you can still afford to be snotty.*

The pair of Avengers aroused the usual curiosity at the inspection table. Onlookers and fellow competitors alike ogled over them from the sidelines. It was the first time even for the officials to see the composite karts.

"This must be the year for originality," the older inspector told Martin. "I understand we're having a new sports car here this weekend also. A home built, constant-velocity drive, called the Bullet, is the buzz."

Martin just frowned, not wanting to elaborate on his Avenger. "Well you know racing is innovation. What we come up with on the racetrack today, trickles into Detroit tomorrow."

The inspector laughed. "If it works that is."

"Yeah…if it works."

The number of sports cars in the paddock equaled the number of karts. It was a healthy mix of racing machinery that covered the whole spectrum of the sport. Friday practice rotated between the two sanctioning bodies. The Kart Association would run its invitational event on Saturday, giving Sunday over to the Sports Car Club for the keynote Grand Prix event. It had the making of a full racing card for everyone.

After safety tech, Brent stood at trackside to watch the sports cars. There was an interesting assortment of full bodied sportsracers and open-wheel, single-seat formulas, the big brother of the sprint and shifter karts.

At precisely 9 o'clock the track opened for combined kart practice, and as usual for the first round, the field was slim. Mac got Martin started first and then he started Brent. Once again it was an entirely new track but the same old anticipation.

When Brent pulled out onto the front straightaway, Hannah eagerly joined him, waving. He decided to slip in behind her and study her racing line. After all, she ran the challenging 2½ mile Heartland road course before and would be an ideal guide.

Turn 1 was a classic right hander that fed into the first of two sets of esses. To add complexity, the Turn 4 hairpin sprang up immediately following a very short chute, allowing little time for readjustment. An observation tower, apparently for spectators, introduced the 5/8 mile backstretch as one continuous, easy arc that provided a moment of rest before entering the tiring back course.

Dust lingered in the air from a previous off-road excursion at the sharp, left hand Turn 5. But Brent noted an ample run-off area in case of forfeiting the turn.

"Expect some excitement here," he told himself as he put it in perspective.

He followed Hannah's outside line under the bridge and into the hard braking Turn 6. She proficiently broke the turn down into two simpler bends with a burst of throttle between them. That approach set her up for Turn 7 that began the climb over the bridge.

Good girl, Brent grinned. *That was perfect.*

Turn 8 was another hard braker at the bottom of the hill. It offered a lot of momentum with a ton of traction and the right set-up for the second set of esses. Again, Hannah led him from the outside edge on a late apex with a wiggle through the esses. The final Turn 11 was wide and flat.

Brent accelerated onto the long front straight just inches from the Quantum's tail as they passed two karts lagging on the inside. *Excellent*, he thought. *Miss Branson, you are awesome.*

He continued to trail her for the several laps remaining, settling in with the flow. He made a mental note of all her turn-in points. He identified where the track seemed to leave him and where it came back again. One very clear and distinct observation was that Hannah Branson was the perfect chauffeur. She was smooth and calculating. Come race time though, he would have to figure out some way to do one better. Avenger could not finish behind Quantum again.

Back at their pit, he and Martin exchanged notes.

"Beware of Turn 5," Martin explained. "It pops up on you after the long, endless arch. Thank goodness for the run-off. I could've lost it big time there."

"So, that was you!" Brent chuckled. "I saw that. Luckily, Hannah took me through there flawlessly. She's good."

"Those Branson's have this course mapped out pretty good," Martin admitted. "Harris has his sit-up matching hubs with the lay-downs. He's going to be a real handful for you, Brent."

"I've been told Quantum has him in their new model just for this event," Brent said.

Mac added his comments. "Yeah, well I think that Colton fella is going to be the force to reckon with. I clocked him. Believe it or not that contraption of his had an easy two seconds on everyone out there."

Martin grabbed a drink from the cooler. "Okay then, we know our target. Let's get to work. I'm going to start with about two more pounds of tire pressure all around. And I'm slipping the clutch 500 rpms."

Brent tied the top of his suit around his waist. "I hung with Hannah the whole time with some to spare. I'm sticking with what I have."

Sports cars rumbled onto the track next. Brent

wandered down pit road in search of his friends, Kimmie and Nate. Although Nate didn't register to race in the Grand Prix, with his growing reputation as an engine builder, he supported his customers who were there to race. Brent found them at the other end of pit road.

Nate had just handed over a freshened motor to a client. "Can I share an observation with you?" he asked Brent. "For what it's worth, the Colton boys are really staking out your karts. I was up late last night finishing a motor after you guys turned in. They were loitering across from you."

"Maybe they're just a pair of night owls."

"Or werewolves on the prowl when everyone else is tucked in," Nate suggested. "I'm just suspicious since you had that throttle incident at Rocky Point."

Brent shook his head. "Branson meddled with our linkage. I don't know how, but it was him. I still owe him one for that. He was hanging around the pits real late that night."

"So were the Coltons," Nate argued. "Let me just say I know Harrison a little bit. He's a straight-up guy. I don't know the Coltons, except that they're awfully peculiar. They keep to themselves almost to a fault. They travel the National circuit. They show up, they kick butt and then they disappear into the landscape."

Brent hugged Kimmie goodbye and headed back toward his pit. He chewed on Nate's words. Yes, Harrison Branson was cocky and highly aggressive. But that made him the hard-line competitor he was. He wanted to win as much as anyone, and who could blame him for that? Hannah once said that he and Brent were much alike. Could Brent have misjudged him?

On his journey through the paddock, he stumbled onto the Colton pit discreetly tucked alongside the fence.

The unattended kart was on wooden saw horses. How could it look so sinister at rest, yet when running be so incredibly fast? Perhaps it was time to finally meet the mysterious brothers.

A low growl interrupted the silence. "What do you want?"

Brent spun to see the two brothers standing behind him. "I'm Brent Lockeman," he said as he extended his hand for a formal introduction.

"I know!" snapped the older of the two. "You're the one with that Avenger monstrosity."

Brent felt his blood pressure spike as he withdrew his offer of a handshake. "You must mean Avenger monocoque. I guess your terminology is just faulty."

"We'll test our terminology on the race track," Colton retorted.

Brent scowled. "Sure, let's do that!" Then he turned and walked away.

CHAPTER 21

THE NUMBER OF KARTS PREPARED TO take practice had grown enough to warrant separate sprint, enduro, and shifter fields. Brent watched at trackside as Martin practiced. Mac's stopwatch revealed a gain of one and a half seconds per lap from his previous outing. Even so, it was expected Martin would make one more adjustment when he returned. It was that small tweak to something somewhere on the kart that made him the former state champion he was.

The sprinters took their turn next. Brent watched as Harrison Branson tore out of the pits in the lead in true Harrison style. But he didn't see Hannah's or Colton's karts among the group.

He was clocking Harrison's lap times when a hand lay on his shoulder. Startled, he spun around.

Kyle Nash had joined him. "Not to question your strategy, Lockeman, seeing how well it served you in the past, but I think you should be more concerned with the Coltons than with Branson. But then, that's just my opinion."

Brent joked. "You're one to talk about strategy serving one well, Mr. Shifter Kart."

Kyle was being serious. "Let me give you something to think about. Why do the Coltons run an extra loop of fuel line around their gas tank before it goes to the carburetor?"

Brent was taken off guard by the strange question. "I give up. Why?"

Kyle looked at him narrowly. "I have my opinion but I won't go there. I have no stake in the matter. It's just something to think about." He waved farewell. "I have to run, my practice is next. Oh, by the way, A.J. sends her best wishes to you."

Brent watched him walk away. What was meant by the fuel line remark and why was he troubled by it? Suddenly he lost interest in timing Harris any longer. He hung the stopwatch from his neck and headed back to the pit.

Hannah met him on pit road. "Hi, Brent. I assume you're all set to race since you aren't in practice."

"You too I take it?"

"Yeah, pretty much. I felt like a walk."

"What a coincidence," Brent responded. "I just thought about picking up a cold drink and taking a stroll myself. Can I offer you an iced tea?"

She beamed with surprise. "My my. I believe that's the first offer you ever made me. How can I refuse? Can I offer to walk with you in return?"

At his canopy, Brent grabbed two teas from the cooler. "I'll be back in a little while Uncle Martin," he called.

As he handed a drink to Hannah, she grabbed his other hand. "Let's go!"

Her babbling was incoherent as Brent gnawed on

what Kyle had laid on him. As they walked together sipping tea, hand in hand, she talked away, yet he barely heard her. He had to somehow get a glimpse of that Colton kart.

The Colton pit was empty as they casually sauntered past. The kart was still on the saw horses but it had since been covered with a small tarp. Brent stopped walking when he got beside it and looked around.

Hannah stopped talking in mid-sentence. "What's up?" she asked confused.

Brent lifted an edge of the tarp. Kyle's observation was correct. "Why do they run an extra loop of fuel line?"

Hannah shook her head. "I don't know. It's not allowed in the specs. The rules forbid the use of any excess fuel line."

Brent released the corner of the tarp and quickly stepped away, guiding Hannah along with him. "Someone else noticed it and brought it to my attention."

Hannah looked back toward the kart. "Harris doesn't trust these guys. He says they're up to no good. I just thought it was him being paranoid all the time." She paused and then giggled. "Actually, he said the same thing about you."

Brent looked at her with a slight annoyance. "If you're referring to that throttle episode at Rocky Point, I'll have you know that wasn't me. My carbs were tampered with also."

Hannah frowned. "So were ours. And yet you accused Harris."

"Okay," Brent conceded. "I admit I may have acted prematurely about that. Uncle Martin says I do that sometimes."

"Your uncle sounds like a wise man. I see why

you're so close." She grabbed his hand in hers again.

"He's like a father to me," Brent explained. "When my father died, he and Aunt Suz stepped in to help my mom and me."

Hannah smiled softly. "I'd like to meet your mom sometime."

Brent shook his head from the thought of it. "Oh, no. No! My Mom and I are too close for that kind of thing."

"Too close for what kind of thing?" She threw a quick look skyward. "Wow. We actually rose to the level where we can share our inner most secrets with each other."

Brent felt a strange shiver go through him. "Inner most secrets? I just told you my dad died and my mom and I grew closer because of it. It's not my biography."

"It's a start," she declared. "It's a nice start."

Brent left Hannah at her pit. Harris was busy replacing tires on his kart and pretended not to notice his sister's company.

Tow vehicles were gathering up the few breakdowns scattered around the course from the last practice as the sports cars filed onto pit lane for their track time next.

"Are you good to go for your race?" Martin asked Brent when he returned. "We'll have one last chance to go out when the sports cars are finished."

"I'm good," Brent replied. "I have nothing to change. I don't want to risk anything out there."

Martin agreed. "Ok. I'm ready for a hot burger from the snack bar. I'm tired of cold ham and cheese sandwiches. Let's all go for a hike."

They sat at a picnic table under an umbrella outside the snack bar to eat. "What would be the advantage of running extra fuel line on the kart," Brent asked.

Martin frowned. "There is none...performance wise anyway. An old trick was to use that extra line to house illegal fuel so it wouldn't mix in the tank. The hot fuel always got you to Turn 1 first but it never registered on the test meter. There was no trace of it after the race."

Brent quietly bit his sandwich.

"Okay," Martin demanded. "What's up, Brent?"

"That explains how the Coltons always lead the first lap," he replied. "So it does have a performance gain... indirectly."

"Brent, you have to stop with all these conspiracy theories," Mac cautioned.

"Kyle Nash brought it to my attention," Brent explained. "Hannah and I just checked out their kart. It's true."

Martin shook his head. "Extra fuel line in itself doesn't prove hot fuel. It's merely an old ploy."

Brent shrugged. "Then perhaps tech should be alerted and do an inspection just to make sure."

Mac disagreed. "You would have to file a formal complaint and pay the fee refundable only if you win your protest. It's not the easiest thing to prove because certain other chemicals can fool the test meter also."

Brent dropped his sandwich on the paper plate. "So we do nothing! We just stand by and let them get away with it!"

Martin laid his hand on his nephew's wrist. "Unless we can prove wrong doing, Brent, they're not getting away with anything. The old adage 'innocent until proven guilty' holds true in racing also."

Brent got up to leave. "Then we'll prove it."

Martin grabbed his arm. "No! We'll watch them.

We'll file the proper protest at the proper time." He released his hold. "Don't run off half loaded on this. Your accusations are serious ones."

"But this is serious, and Hannah agrees."

Martin stared deep into Brent's eyes. "Brent, there are some things you need to get in check. Hannah Branson is a nice girl, but she's also a worthy competitor. Don't let your guard down."

The snack area was still bustling with activity when they left.

Martin took advantage of the last afternoon kart practice. He roared out of the pits in the midst of forty-four other enduros. Brent leaned over the top of pit wall to watch the concentrated horde shuffle around Turn 1.

Suddenly, chaos struck. Body pieces erupted into the air. A blue kart barrel-rolled onto the grass run-off. Hunks of plastic, rubber and sod blended above it like a galactic storm cloud.

Everyone on pit road stretched to see what had just transpired. Brent stood on top of the wall to get a better look. He was horrified by what he saw. The Avenger was upside down on top of Martin.

The red flag waved vigorously from the flag stand as turn workers rushed the corner. Brent jumped from the wall and ran as fast as he could down the track with Mac in close pursuit. The medic truck sped out of the pits with lights flashing and sirens blaring.

By the time Brent reached the scene, Martin was standing on the grass, grasping his left shoulder. A medical attendant was examining his neck and chest area, while another medic tended to a second driver involved. Parked karts were being directed back to the pits in order to clear the area of debris.

"What the blazes happened?" Mac yelled to

Martin above the commotion.

Martin's jaw tightened. "The rear locked up right in the middle of the turn."

Brent sought clarification. "Your brakes locked?"

"No!" Martin corrected. "I mean the axle locked up. I was on the throttle, there was a sudden jerk, and the kart came around on me."

Wide-eyed and confused, Brent looked down at the kart, now resting upright. The wheel hub slid all the way in on the axle and was lodged against the bearing pocket.

Completing their spot examination, the medics concurred to transport Martin to the local hospital for X-rays. Mac was instructed to ride along as the accompanying adult. While the clean-up continued on the racetrack, Brent rode with the flat trailer to deliver the Avenger back to the pit.

Nate and Kimmie were already there waiting, along with a small crowd of bystanders which included both of the Bransons.

Kimmie was tearfully emotional. "Is Mr. Kessick going to be alright?"

"He seems to be bruised somewhat," Brent answered. "The medics want X-rays just to make sure there's nothing more serious."

Nate helped to lift the kart from the trailer.

"I don't get this," Brent grumbled. "I checked that wheel hub myself. It was fine."

Nate knelt down to inspect it more closely. "The locking bolt is loose. The hub bound against the frame."

Brent felt tension form in his stomach. "How could the pinch bolt come loose? What's going on here, Nate? The things that are happening don't just happen on their own."

"It wouldn't take much to free a pinch bolt," Nate answered. "Walk by for five seconds when no one is looking and bingo, a couple of turns with an Allen wrench and it's done. Then keep on walking."

"You're not saying what I think you're saying...are you?" Brent proposed.

"Was the kart out in the open unattended at all?"

Brent considered the query. "Lunch. We went to the snack bar for lunch. Both karts were sitting here."

By the time practice restarted the small crowd that gathered had long dispersed. Nate and Kimmie remained. And to Brent's surprise, so did Hannah.

"Well, this thing won't see the track again," Nate surmised as they further inspected the kart. "The composite is cracked at several reinforcements, both front spoilers are shattered and the steering arms are bent."

"We needed that race tomorrow," Brent grumbled. "Now both Uncle Martin and the Enduro are out."

Nate was more optimistic. "You have a roller sitting over there. We'll throw this running gear on it and race that one. Isn't that why you brought the spares along anyway?"

"Did I just hear you volunteer to help?" Brent mused.

"Sure. I'll give you a hand," Nate said. "Get them both up on stands side by side. We'll swap everything from one chassis to the other."

"I don't think Mr. Kessick will be in any shape to drive it tomorrow," Kimmie reasoned, still emotional.

Brent addressed that dilemma firmly. "Then I will."

Hannah finally spoke, but her demeanor was grave. "Brent, you can't be serious about running your uncle's race right before you run your own. That would be torture. You won't make it through both. Harris thinks you're enough of a hazard as it is."

Brent stepped around her toward the tool chest. "Then be sure to tell him to stay out of my way."

CHAPTER 22

THE TRANSFORMATION FROM ROLLER to racer went smooth and swift. Nate replaced the sparkplug wire that got ripped off during the flip-over and installed the engine onto the roller. Brent installed the axle clutch and bled the brakes. Then he swapped the display wheels and tires with the new Malta racing set.

All lines were connected and linkages adjusted when Mac and Martin returned from the hospital in the medic truck.

Martin's left arm was in a sling. "Shoulder separation," was all he told his inquisitive audience.

"Nothing broken?" Brent questioned. "No ribs, or arms or rotator cuff? Uncle Martin, you took a heck of a spill out there."

"Shoulder separation," Martin repeated. "Doc said no racing for at least a month. I suppose that nails it for Enduro this weekend."

"Not if we can help it," Brent spewed. "That's why we brought the spares."

"Brent, we're packing it in for the enduro. We

have to concentrate on the sprinter tomorrow. We may have a spare kart but we don't have a spare driver."

"I'm driving it!"

"You have to focus on your own race," Martin insisted. "I'm not going to ask you to run two full races in the same afternoon."

"You're not asking…I already decided. We have the enduro all ready to go."

Mac cut in the conversation. "Brent, we need you to be spot on your game tomorrow. Don't jeopardize our whole weekend by stretching yourself that far. We have to salvage something from all our effort. And it looks like you're it."

"I have this covered," Brent argued. "I can do it."

Martin disagreed. "No! You haven't turned a single lap in that kart. You can't expect to go out there cold and prove anything."

"It'll serve as a warm-up run for my own race," Brent insisted. "I ran a lay-down before, remember?"

"That was two years ago," Martin reminded him.

"Let me use it as one last practice run for this course," Brent pleaded. "It'll just happen in your race. No pressure, just practice."

Martin could not continue the wrangle. The look of pain was all over his face. He turned and disappeared inside the trailer. Mac took one glance at the converted roller-now-racer and retreated to the trailer behind him.

Kimmie approached Brent with open arms and hugged him. "Are you sure you're up to this?"

Brent huffed. "I think I just need a good night's sleep. Thanks for your help Nate."

Nate motioned for Kimmie to follow him away. "Yeah, I just hope now I won't be sorry."

Saturday morning came early for Brent. He was

up before Mac or Martin. He fought his anxiety by trying to convince himself he had a quality night's sleep. But that was seldom the case on a race day.

The paddock overflowed with the commotion and smell of a Grand Prix race. The agenda was loaded. It was media day. It was last chance, hardship practice and qualifying day for the sports cars. It was the Kart Association Invitational Race day. Spectators were already filing through the gates.

Paranoid about his recent measure of bad luck, Brent worked half of the morning going over both karts with a jeweler's eye. He checked and double-checked all bolts, lines, pressures and adjustments. Nate's reference to their unattended karts disturbed him. He could not afford to take anything for granted anymore. That was evident by Martin's upset down in Turn 1 the previous day.

It was Brent's escape before a race to find an observation area and try to relax. He would study the varying strategies taken through a particular part of the race course; the brake points, entries and exits. He found such information to be therapeutic. It relieved the anxiety that accompanied the wait for the race itself. And to study the racing line of sports cars could be quite helpful.

When he stepped onto pit road his hand was grabbed from behind. "Hi, Brent," Hannah greeted. "How is your uncle doing?" The top half of her purple and yellow driver's suit was tied around her waist.

"He's okay...sore, sour and sassy...but okay."

"So, who do we spy on this time?"

Brent shrugged to mask his intention. "How about if we spy on the sports cars in the esses as they come off the hill?"

"Sounds good to me. I'm with you."

It was a leisurely fifteen minute walk from the paddock to the Turn 8 bleachers. They watched the racers qualifying as they walked along the wooden country fence that meandered along the race track. Once at the bleachers they sat down together on the bottom bench, all alone.

They had only observed a couple of cars when a man and woman joined them on the bench. The man was on crutches and apparently stopped to rest his leg.

"Hi there," Hannah welcomed, to break the silence.

"Hi," the man replied. "I'm Russ Thorton with Bullet Racing." He acknowledged Hannah's suit. "I see you race the karts. I've seen them around at various tracks. Impressive little machines."

Brent recognized the Bullet reference. "I'm Brent Lockeman with Avenger Karts. So, that's your car, the Bullet, which had everyone buzzing yesterday? There was a big write-up in *Competition News* floating all around the track about it."

Russ chuckled. "Yeah. It's been a little crazy lately. But if you want to build a better product, you have to build a different product. Otherwise, it's just a copy."

Brent grinned. "Man, you sound just like my Uncle Martin. We've been taking the same kind of raspberries with our Avenger. I'm running it in the Kart Association Invitational this afternoon."

"Well then, Mr. Lockeman," Russ said. "Here's to the both of us setting all those nay-sayers straight." They exchanged high-five slaps. "That's my kind of spirit."

The woman sat down and smiled at Hannah. "I'm Holli Thorton. I'm with Bullet Racing too. So, are you with the Avenger team also?"

Hannah stood up. "Oh my no! I'm Hannah Branson. I drive a Quantum kart. Brent and I are just friendly competitors."

Brent rolled his eyes. "Formidable is more like it. This girl is awesome on the racetrack."

Hannah smiled and bent down to rub her nose with his. "You're pretty hot yourself, young man."

Holli winked at Russ and looked at Hannah. "You hang in there," she smiled. "There is hope in this man's world for us women." Then she helped Russ up the bleachers to the top bench.

Brent watched Russ hobble up the rows of seats. "I can't imagine the dedication he must have to build and race a car of his own design at that level."

Hannah sat back down beside him. "What do you mean you can't imagine? You seem to have it covered pretty well."

Brent stared at an open-wheel formula car blasting through Turn 8 in front of them and considered his circumstances; the sweat, the finances and the bad luck. "Yeah, we have it covered alright," he mumbled. He never was comfortable with a lie.

Hannah leaned in close. "What's the matter?" she asked somberly. "All of a sudden you like...just shut down."

Brent gazed into her eyes. They radiated the same enticing glow as they did that night on the hotel bench at Rocky Point. Before he could help it he leaned forward and kissed her.

She didn't flinch even when he pulled away. She just stared at him, blinking, and her stance never waned.

He blushed. He was never that impetuous before and he wasn't sure how to explain what he had just done. He searched for words...a couple of words...even one word to justify it, but he found none. After the hush finally got to him he stammered, "I owed you that."

Though he sensed her mouth twitch, Hannah remained silent.

The silence was too awkward. "We should probably be heading back," Brent said. "I have some races to run."

"You really are going to attempt both races aren't you?" Hannah asked.

Brent stood up to leave. "I have to!"

"I'm not so sure. Do you have to, or do you think you have to?"

Hannah chatted disjointedly on the way back to the pits. Brent wasn't sure if she was reacting to his impulsive advance at her or his zealous ambition to run both races. But whatever the reason, he barely heard a word she said. The reality of his impulsiveness had overcome him.

Mac and Martin were having a hearty conversation beside the Avengers with a visitor when Brent stepped under the canopy at his pit. The man had a long-lens camera dangling from his neck and a satchel slung over his shoulder.

"Hello!" voiced the young, lanky guest when he saw Brent. "I'm Trevor Daniels with *Competition News*. I'm covering the Grand Prix for my paper. While you were gone, your partners here agreed to some photo ops."

Brent shook his hand. "I'm Brent Lockeman. I'll be driving the two karts."

"Yes, that's what I've been told," Trevor acknowledged. "The controversy you've created here will make an interesting story for our readers. This must be the week for originality." He clutched his camera. "Well, thank you gentlemen. Now if you'll excuse me, I have to run. I have a lot to cover yet."

When he left, Mac exhaled excitedly. "He said he'll run a cover story on the Avenger like he did with the new Bullet race car. That story is flying all over the place this weekend."

"Yeah, I heard," Brent informed them. "We just met the Bullet people over on the bleachers."

"Who's we?" Martin asked.

"Me and Hannah. We were checking out the sports cars going into the esses."

Martin looked at Mac and shook his head.

The conversation switched topics several times as they ate lunch and waited for the sports cars to complete their qualifying.

CHAPTER 23

IT WAS A COUPLE OF MINUTES BEFORE 3 o'clock in the afternoon. The sports cars finished qualifying on time at 2:30 and Heartland Motor Speedway transformed into Grand Prix mode. Brent was lying in the Avenger Enduro on the starting grid.

It was a three-split start, with 2-cycle Opens in the lead group, 100cc Yamaha in the middle and 4-cycle Briggs in the third group. Since Brent was a last minute change of driver and in a substitute entry, he was assigned to the tail end of his class in the middle group.

"Nowhere to go but up," Brent joked to Mac kneeling and ready with the starter beside him.

"Don't make me regret I permitted this," Mac grumbled. "This is just a practice run for you, remember? Save your energy and any heroics for your own race."

A.J. Barlett and Kyle Nash were standing hand-in-hand behind pit wall to watch the enduros start. A.J. called to Brent. "Be careful out there, and good luck." She was smiling keenly. "This reminds me of you and me at the 3 Hour Silva two years ago."

Brent nodded. On many levels that seemed like a lifetime ago.

When the green flag chopped through the air from the other side of the track, the first of the three groups blasted off in an ear-piercing orchestra of open exhausts.

Brent propped his head against the padding of the headrest and sighted through the crescent steering wheel. Mac spun the starter motor. Vroom!

Stomach knotted and fingers clenched. Then the flag sliced for the second start.

The Avenger sprung toward the flagman and left two karts in its wake. It rode the outer edge all the way to Turn 1 as it passed four more karts. Brent squirmed in his reclined position to get his reflexes in check. All he could see was a jumbled maze.

As the field channeled into rows of two-by-two for the first bend, Brent coaxed himself, *Settle down now and get the feel of this thing. This is practice. No pressure.*

The pack glided around the turn as if riding on a set of rails. Through the esses and the hairpin, everyone maintained their place. Once on the endless arc of the backstretch however, the formation split up. Karts scurried for a change of position.

Brent stabbed the accelerator to see what the Avenger would do. It overtook three more karts before the tachometer digits stopped prancing.

"Wow," was all he could muster.

Turn 5 created a bottle-neck that continued through the tunnel all the way to the incline. Brent passed two more karts going over the bridge. But that was the last of the back pack. Up ahead the front group was pulling away.

He settled himself in. *Let the real racing begin.*

It took until the start-finish line to close up on his

next two victims. He wedged himself between them and they rounded Turn 1 three abreast. He inched ahead of them through the esses and was fully clear storming out of the hairpin.

Three karts were off the track at Turn 6, but Brent couldn't tell which of the three classes they were in. He would have to wait for a pit signal to find out how they affected him, if at all.

His answer came as he passed the pits. Mac flashed him a large '7' on the pit board.

Seventh place. Thank you. Brent signaled with a raised hand as he went past. The Avenger did well cutting through the early field.

Nothing changed for several laps. Then the yellow flag came out at Turn 5 for two laps. And then a couple of laps later, two karts were sitting in the grass along the spectator tower near the hairpin.

Brent checked over his gauges. The exhaust temperature had still not reached normal. So while on the front straight, he closed the hi-speed needle an eighth of a turn to lean out the fuel mixture.

The temperature response was instant, as was the power output. Before he reached the tunnel he had all but eradicated the distance to the sixth place kart. By the time he crossed over the bridge, he was tapping its rear bar. But it took him until the front straightaway to complete the pass. His rival blocked him at every attempt.

Mac's next signal read…'MID'.

The race had reached the midpoint. Brent hadn't realized until then that his arms were getting heavy, and he still had another thirty minutes to go. His neck grew stiffer as the laps sped by and the headrest was giving him a cramp. He wasn't used to lying on his back and looking through the steering wheel to see the road ahead. He wanted to do his combat sitting upright. But it was his decision to drive the enduro so he would bear with it just as he had done before.

He eventually edged his way up to the leaders; a group of three battling for third place, and a separate duo ahead of them fighting for first.

He studied the trio directly ahead. They displayed no consistency in style or function. Each tempted the others in a ruthless bid for third place. Their constant shuffling left no opportunity for Brent to advance. He tailed them, lying in wait, perched for an opening.

When the pit board read 'GO' he knew Mac meant it was the final lap. He would have to strike with one last challenge.

He noted earlier in the hairpin of a common flaw in his adversaries; they each left the inside wide open. The inside meant a tighter, slower groove but if executed properly, it could provide him with a triple pass. He figured it was worth the risk.

He positioned himself accordingly for the final lap. Then he entered the hairpin off the racing line and powered to the inside. As he predicted, the lane was open.

Tires howled under heavy braking, but the Avenger clung diligently to the absolute edge. As Brent attempted to initiate a square corner, his three foes tried to circle him on the outside. He scooted through, clutching to the edge, and aimed for the backstretch.

He passed two of his rivals and roared toward Turn 5 tied for third place. The digits on his tachometer danced sporadically on the screen as he inched ahead.

From on top of the bridge, Brent could see the two leaders slither through the second set of esses. Although he knew he couldn't catch them entirely, he was still gaining as he thundered beneath the checkered flag.

His first chance to hear the track announcer was at the weight scales after his cool down lap. "...and young Brent Lockeman, driving the new Avenger Racing entry, advanced from last spot to take home a remarkable third place finish in the 100cc Yamaha class here today."

He was surprised to find the reception committee that was waiting for him at the scales; Uncle Martin, Aunt Suz, his mother and Bobby Wheeling.

He was barely out of the seat when Katherine threw her arms around him. "I don't know if I should congratulate you or scold you young man." She embraced him elatedly.

"Mom!" Brent exclaimed. "What are you guys doing here?"

Martin had a cold drink waiting for him as soon as he cleared the scales.

Bobby Wheeling patted Brent on the shoulder. "I told you I would see she got out to your races. That was a thrill to watch."

"So you saw the race?"

"We saw about the last half," Katherine explained. "Suz got a call from Mac last night about Marty's accident. She was leaving this morning to come down here and we had to come with her."

Aunt Suz took her turn hugging Brent. "I believe it's time someone started watching over you boys. Mac assured me Marty was okay but I still laid awake all night worrying."

Brent frowned. "Now you sound like Mom."

Just then Hannah stepped in and grabbed his arm. "Brent, we're forming on the grid now for Sprints. Are you still up for this?"

Katherine appeared stunned. "Brent, introduce

your friend." But before he got the chance, she greeted Hannah herself. "Hello, I don't believe we've met before. I'm Katherine Lockeman, Brent's mother."

Hannah smiled as they shook hands. "Hi, Mrs. Lockeman. I'm Hannah Branson. Brent and I race in the same class. It's nice to finally meet you."

Katherine glanced back and forth between her and Brent with a look of confusion. "What do you mean, finally?"

Brent had to change the topic, quickly. "Mom, don't start. Hannah is a good friend and an excellent competitor." He turned back to Hannah. "I'm on my way there as soon as I go through the scales. I have to get my kart."

Hannah laughed. "Brent, I'm surprised at you."

Katherine's eyebrows elevated as she repeated the statement. "Brent, I'm surprised at you."

Martin knew a subject change was necessary. "Mac took your kart to the grid awhile, just in case you still want to run. But first I need to know if you feel up to this…and I mean no bull."

Brent masked his stiff neck, heavy arms and developing headache. It was the first chance he had to fully analyze his condition. "I'm fine, Uncle Martin."

Hannah tugged his arm. "Come on then. We'll be starting shortly."

Brent went across the scales with the kart. Then he grabbed the drink from Martin and hastily followed Hannah toward the grid, away from the questioning stares of those around him.

CHAPTER 24

WHEN THEY WERE ALONE ON PIT road, Hannah squeezed Brent's hand. "Brent, you just ran a grueling hour long race. How can you get right back out there?"

Brent worried too many people saw through his cover-up. "Uncle Martin's lay-down race was like a practice for me. It prepared me for my own race." He hoped it sounded convincing enough to her. He barely convinced himself.

Before they arrived at the grid, commotion had already developed at the head of the Yamaha line. A crowd of on-lookers gathered around two race officials at the Colton kart. A tech inspector was conducting an in-line fuel check.

Hannah tightened her squeeze on Brent's hand. "Harrison filed a protest asking for a pre-race fuel test on the Coltons. When I told him what you and I found he went ballistic. He always suspected something was afoul with those guys."

The Coltons argued with the officials, vigorously

attempting to make some point, but to no avail. Their kart was pulled from the grid.

As the crowd opened to make way for their kart's removal, the Coltons' rage grew more heated. Nevertheless, the officials guided their kart of many colors behind the armor rail.

A faint murmuring and applause rippled down the grid. Obviously there was ample support for the decision of the officials.

Brent and Hannah met up with Mac at the Avenger. "Now, that was quite a sight," Brent related.

Mac frowned. "You just witnessed that honesty isn't a virtue with some folks. Your sins will find you out. It says so in the good book."

Just then Brent noticed a decal on the side panel of his kart, a colorful logo that had not been there before. 'Wheeling Properties'. He pointed guardedly. "What is that?"

Mac was prompt with his response. "We were apprised just this morning that Avenger Racing has acquired sponsorship. It appears Mr. Wheeling has an interest in our program. He brought a set of logos with him for immediate exposure."

With the fatigue and mounting headache, Brent wasn't in a frame of mind to think clearly. "Wait a minute. Are you saying Bobby is going to bank-roll us?" He tried to validate his thoughts.

"If by Bobby you mean Robert Wheeling, then yes, that would be accurate."

"When did this all happen?" Brent demanded.

"It's my understanding he and Marty have discussed it for a week or more. I was informed of it last night when I called Suz about Marty's accident. It was finalized when they arrived earlier. You were out on..."

He was interrupted by the blaring of the PA system. "All drivers, there is a mandatory meeting at the tower in five minutes. All drivers must report immediately to the tower for a special meeting to take place in five minutes. Yes drivers, this means you!"

Brent sensed a wave of perplexity seize him. He felt he was fading fast. Too much was coming at him at once. He would have to get the events of the moment under control in his mind if he was to throw himself into another demanding race. He needed to concentrate. He needed a headache pill. But how could he get a headache pill without letting on?

"Hannah," he whispered. "This is all too crazy. You wouldn't happen to have an aspirin on you would you?" He faked a chuckle to mask his seriousness.

"The medic truck is parked by the tower," she replied, nonchalantly. "They would have aspirins."

Of course, he thought to himself. He knew that. And under different circumstances he would have thought of that himself. He sensed a trace of relief. "You're such a doll."

She looked at him passively. "Do you mean you're just now figuring that out all by yourself?"

He washed down the pill with the drink Martin gave him at the weight scales. The maneuver went unnoticed and in time for the meeting to commence. The Race Director explained the details surrounding the disqualification of the Colton kart. The wordy specifics and the accompanying warnings were incoherent to Brent in his frame of mind, although he already knew the core details. After all, he felt as if he and Hannah were somewhat responsible.

The meeting concluded with the drivers being released to their karts waiting on the grid. Hannah still held the squeeze on Brent's hand. She clutched it even tighter when she saw Harris Branson coming toward them.

His piercing glare never waned from Brent. "Hannah, go to your kart awhile. I have something to say to Lockeman here."

It was stated as a command and Hannah resented it. "If I can't hear whatever you need to say, Harris, then maybe it's not worth saying."

His mouth tensed as he pointed a finger at Brent. "I've been watching you get too chummy with my sister all weekend. I told you to stay away from her."

Hannah stepped toward her brother. "Stop it Harris! I choose who I hang out with, not you."

He drilled Brent with insolence. "I just took care of the Colton problem. If you get in my way on the track like you have before, I'll take care of you too."

Creases tightened in Brent's jaw. "You don't scare me Harris. You can't take care of me...you're not man enough."

Insult and anger washed over Harrison's face. Without warning, he lunged forward to grab at Brent's collar, but his attack was intercepted from behind. Kyle Nash stepped from behind and restrained him.

"Didn't you just hear the Director's spiel about zero tolerance, Branson?" Kyle charged. "Stand down!"

Harris flung off the hold on him. "I have zero tolerance with the track antics of this menace and his moving in on my sister."

Kyle shook his head. "Your sister is a big girl Harris. It's time you realize that. And let me just say, I went up against Brent in the past. He's a straight-up guy. Yes, he is aggressive, but then the very same has been said about you."

Harris backed away. "He just did a full stint out there, Nash. He can't be in any rational shape to be back on that race track."

"That's not your call," Kyle replied. "There's nothing in the rules to prevent it. Besides, for all you know, his vigor may be all spent by now." He paused before adding one final point. "My race follows you guys. Keep it on the up-and-up out there. I don't want my race delayed while they have to clean up your mess."

Harris started to walk around Kyle, and then turned to point at Brent one last time. "Stay out of my way out there Lockeman."

Brent huffed. "Is that a threat?"

"I don't make threats. Call it a warning."

"Then I suggest the same warning to you."

Harris stormed off toward the grid and Kyle turned to leave.

"I didn't need your protection, Kyle," Brent protested.

Kyle stopped and grinned at him. "I wasn't protecting you from Branson, Lockeman. I was protecting Branson from you."

Hannah smiled faintly at Brent. "I know from your perspective this is hard to believe, but Harris really isn't all that bad. He takes competition very, very serious. Keep a cool head and don't let him get to you. Put him behind you."

"That's exactly what Uncle Martin tells me all the time."

Hannah laughed. "I really have to get to know your folks." After what seemed to be an awkward pause, she gave him a quick kiss on the cheek. "I suppose now you'll owe me another one." She turned to leave. "Good luck in your second race...and be safe. I'll be out there with you…watching."

Martin and Mac were addressing an inquisitive audience surrounding the Avenger when Brent returned to the grid.

"I would like very much to talk to this Hannah friend of yours," Katherine said as she put her arm on Brent's shoulder. "She seems like a sweet girl."

Brent's state of mind was too inundated for a plausible response. "Yeah, she's alright," he blurted, after which he felt no response at all may have been better.

The PA speakers rumbled. "Attention in the pits. Non-racing personnel must leave the grid. The flag for the Sprint classes will go up in five minutes. The next race is about to commence. I repeat, all non-racing personnel please clear the grid area immediately."

Katherine hugged Brent and placed a kiss on his forehead. "Please be careful out there, Son." As she stroked his face, he felt a cold metal band rub his cheek.

He lifted her hand. An engagement ring, sparkling and reflective, crowned her finger. He studied it quietly and then threw a glance at the logos on the side of his Avenger. "Wow, Mom," he murmured. "Bobby was busy with the checkbook lately I see."

She pulled away. "We'll talk about that another time. For now young man, you keep your mind on the racetrack."

CHAPTER 25

AS THE FIRST GROUP TORE FROM THE grid, the flagman repositioned himself to release the second group, Brent's group. Three groups…again, three groups of hungry predators ready to strike.

Brent exhaled a calming breath. Just more than one hour earlier, he sat on that very grid, knotted stomach, dry mouth. Just an hour earlier though seemed like an era; he was raring and anxious. But this time he was tired and sore. His neck ached, his arms hunkered and his head still throbbed. He felt sensitive pressure points on his body he didn't even know existed. Yet if he dare let it show he knew he would be yanked from the grid by his mother, his uncle, certainly by Harrison Branson, and perhaps even Hannah. Suddenly the aspirin he took didn't seem like enough.

Engines growled up and down the line.

Mac spun the motor. Vroom! Avenger joined in the chorus of ringing exhausts. The much awaited Southern Grand Prix…the much anticipated Avenger christening…was about to become history. What would the pages of time record for either?

The flag snapped. A world of serenity swept behind as a new world unfolded ahead.

Brent dove immediately for his instinctive outside groove, but it was occupied. He was engulfed in the surge of the masses, absorbed by the havoc of confusion.

The Avenger took a hit on the right side and a jolt from behind. *Welcome to the green flag shuffle*, Brent thought. He squeezed the steering wheel and settled in for the long haul...the hour long haul.

The double flash of yellow and purple in Turn 1 confirmed the Quantum team amidst the front of the pack. There was a lot of pavement between them and the Avenger, a lot of competition to conquer.

Brent was the fulcrum of a side-by-side threesome through Turn 1, the esses and into the hairpin. He was pinned in a box with no open road, no escape. Despite the nuisance of a rhythmic headache, he knew he had to at least equal the performance of those around him for any hope of advancement.

Stringing out of the field began on the backstretch. There the turmoil finally found some sense of order. By Turn 5 Brent had unloaded the pair that had him boxed in and he had invaded the ranks of a foursome ahead. But farther ahead still the actual leaders were already through the underpass.

Having just spent the past hour on the course, Brent felt a certain kinship with the track, an advantage he hoped to capitalize on.

He gambled and pressed deeper into the turn before braking, deeper than his opponents. Unwinding to the outside he roared under the bridge and into Turn 6 all by himself. He couldn't count the karts ahead, but he knew they would be the toughest on the track. And they were pulling away. He had to concede they all were refreshed while he was near exhaustion.

From atop the bridge he could see the leaders down below in the esses, the margin between them slightly shrinking. That was encouraging, if only in his mind. He felt his vigor returning. Unlike the enduro, the sprinter was more his type. It made the bullish task seem easier.

With confidence on the rise, he slipped smoothly past two karts on the front straight and another on the inside of Turn 1. A pair of racers sat off-course out of the hairpin near the spectator tower but he couldn't tell which class they were in.

The yellow caution flag waved in Turn 8 for two more karts, but again he couldn't determine their class. All alone he trailed the lead group past the pits where he received his first signal from Mac…'7'.

That confirmed his suspicions. The six-pack ahead was all part of his class. For two laps he nipped away at the gap. Though they scrambled haphazardly among themselves, the group stayed intact but out of reach. Again, Brent conceded they were agile while he was worn; they were fresh while he was depleted. Perhaps Kyle was right earlier, that his vigor was all used up.

He hung back for a couple of laps to allow the field to sort itself out and give himself a second breath. Through the battle up ahead, Brent noticed Harris had taken over the lead…where Harris Branson always had to be. Twin sister Hannah had been shuffled to the rear.

So Brent chipped away at her for two laps. He finally caught her on the back straight where she dropped out of the lead formation and struggled to hold her own.

He moved out to pass her but then reconsidered

and swung back into her slipstream. He nudged her push bar to let her know he initiated a draft. A flash of her gloved hand acknowledged she knew he was there.

The reward of their co-op effort was evident on the front straightaway when they infiltrated the lead pack again.

By wrestling with one another for positions, the leaders sacrificed something more precious, a getaway. They merely insulated Harrison Branson from any viable challenge. And Harris was a master at capitalizing on such an opportunity. He extended his lead with each lap of the racecourse. He had to be stopped.

Brent mulled over whether to abandon Hannah and invade the leaders on his own, or continue to hang with her and hope that together they prevail. But he had to admit, she was getting the job done. She was smooth and methodical. It was her guidance, turn-by-turn, that moved them up into the lead pack. After all, Brent was tired. Could he even do it on his own?

The next pit board read…'MID'…short and to the point.

Brent knew he had to hang on to be within striking distance at the end and Hannah could make that happen. Anticipation mounted. His dependence was on Hannah Branson to pull him through.

"Come on girl," he muttered inside his face shield. "I really will owe you one."

They eliminated two of the leaders after two laps of dicing. Hannah found just the right line through the corners to pull herself and Brent through. On the long straights she sliced the air so he could push them both through. They each knew what the other had to do. Brent occasionally tapped the Quantum's push bar to assure Hannah he was still back there.

Karts were displaced all around the race course. But the four most important to Brent were all in his sight up ahead. And at some point he would have to deal with the fact that Hannah was one of them.

She made her bid on the third place kart by stealing the inside on Turn 7. Up the incline, the pair roared over the bridge side by side, and then down into the hard braking Turn 8.

But her adversary held his line for the inside and Hannah couldn't complete the pass. Pinched to the outside, she desperately fought to stay on course. They both overshot the turn.

Brent backed off to give them the room they needed. Scorching rubber squealed on lock-up. The Quantum skidded onto the run-off area and the other kart followed with a full spin.

Brent threw his kart off the inside edge to avoid contact and launched toward the esses in a blinding cloud of dust. He bounced back onto the pavement with a jolt but was clear of the turmoil. Over his shoulder he saw the yellow flag waving to slow down those entering the turn behind him. Up ahead he saw the second place kart enter Turn 11 and Harrison's Quantum exit it.

Suddenly his fatigue returned with a vengeance. He had forgotten it. The aftershock of Race 1 had been shrouded by all the mental strain of battle. But with Hannah out of contention, he was on his own. It was up to the Avenger to pull him through.

The pit board read...'3'.

Brent knew that. Couldn't Mac see he had the two leaders in sight? He wanted something more from his pit than that. He wanted advice. He wanted suggestions. He wanted a miracle.

He hurled into Turn 1 on his own again. The

Avenger felt good on its own. It was stable and sure-footed. He realized he hadn't experienced it in the race like he should have. He hadn't applied it under its own merit. He spent the race trailing Hannah, compromised. It was time to see what Avenger could really do.

He locked his sights on the second place kart and forged through the esses and the hairpin. He stomped the accelerator. The Avenger chewed up the track and demanded more.

He had his opponent reeled in by the end of the backstretch. Copying Hannah's smooth driving style, he thundered past without a challenge and soared over the bridge in second place.

Hannah waved to him from the grass as he rounded Turn 8. The yellow caution flag was gone.

His focus was on the purple and yellow Quantum ahead. It was crunch time, D-Day, Armageddon. It was time to see what Harrison Branson was really made of...or perhaps Brent Lockeman.

The pit board simply read...'GO'.

"I got it!" Brent grinned. But after almost two hours of intense competition, it even hurt to grin.

For two laps he studied his nemesis, the race leader. He studied his technique and his attitude. As he did so, one thing was obvious; his technique and his attitude had become sloppy. Harris realized Brent was closing in.

In two laps they caught the back runners and Brent was in striking distance. Although the track was congested, Harris slipped through the traffic like an eel in water, and Brent followed in his wake.

The Avenger responded to every demand, matching everything the Quantum had. Brent hoped for just one flaw in Harris's performance, the simplest

182

misjudgment that he could exploit. But it would have to happen soon if he was to have anything left in him to answer the call. His zeal was fading fast.

It came at the hairpin on the final lap. A straggling kart held the racing line and Harris circled wide expecting momentum to sling him past.

Brent set up for a late apex entry. Well past the center of the turn he dove for the inside. Side-by-side the trio blasted onto the backstretch together. A drag race ensued past the spectator tower and around the long arc. The Quantum inched ahead on the left of the lapped kart while the Avenger inched ahead on the right.

Bearing down on Turn 5, Harris had the coveted groove. He nudged to the right to steal some room but Brent squeezed the steering wheel and held him to his line.

Both karts squealed in protest under locked braking and skidded wildly into the bend trying to find grip. The Avenger found it first, jerked to the left into the side of the Quantum, and drug it along into the turn.

Locked together as one they screamed under the bridge. Harris steered frantically to shake free from Brent while Brent wrestled to free himself from Harris. Turn 6. Turn 7. Up the hill and over the bridge, neither one let up.

Brent finally regained the inside line on Turn 8. At his turn-in point a jolt from his determined foe startled him. The Avenger teetered on the edge of traction. To avoid a spin he threw his kart off the inside edge like he did only a few laps earlier when Hannah skidded onto the grass.

The Avenger bounced back onto the pavement at the same spot as before and into the side of the Quantum. Through the esses, around Turn 11 and down the front straight they were a single entity. Both drivers crouched low in their seat with the checkered flag looming in the distance.

Spectators, karters and sports car fans alike pressed against the fence lining the long stretch to the finish line. Three separate classes were on the race course, yet all eyes were on the two leading Yamahas. Pit wall was a blurred streak of colors.

The Avenger sliced beneath the chopping flag barely leading by a front wheel.

CHAPTER 26

HARRIS SLAPPED THE STEERING wheel with his open hand, unwilling to look in Brent's direction. Brent slumped from the overwhelming stress that invaded his body. It was like the Silva 3 Hour Endurance finale all over again; the cool-down lap, the cheering trackside fans and the burst of inner emotions not yet fully comprehended.

He circled the race course, returning the waves of his stranded fellow racers and the spectators. Hannah waved excitedly as he rounded Turn 8, after learning the outcome at the finish line from the PA system.

Between the three classes exiting the race track and the shifter karts taking over the grid, pit road was a mad house.

Brent progressed steadily to the scales, dodging any possible interference from the rushing fans. He could not allow a technicality to infringe on the finish.

Kyle Nash welcomed him at the weight scales in full race gear for his shifter race. "Lockeman, I swear, you are totally unbelievable." He helped Brent out of the kart. "You just pulled another ace out of that deck of yours…again. Congrats man."

He helped push the Avenger across the scales and then behind pit wall. "Hey, I gotta run. I don't want them sending the shifters off without me." As he backed away to leave he pointed a finger at Brent. "We need to talk about Avenger Shifter."

"Avenger Racing doesn't have a shifter," Brent yelled above the ruckus around him.

"That's what we need to talk about," Kyle yelled back as he swung around and rushed toward the grid.

Mac finally got through the crowd with the push stick, along with Katherine and Bobby Wheeling.

Katherine threw her arms around Brent with a sparkle of joy in her eyes. "Honey, I said it worries me how you've grown up so fast. But after seeing today how you handle yourself out there, I don't think I have to worry anymore." She kissed him on the cheek. "I am so proud of you."

Bobby patted him on the back. "I have to say, I am very impressed with that kart of yours, my boy." He caught his slip-up by the stares thrown his way. "Ah, I mean, Brent."

Uncle Martin and Aunt Suz pushed through the congestion. Martin shook Brent's hand with his good arm. "I can't believe it. You actually pulled off both races. Man, talk about confidence."

Mac took over pushing the Avenger to the trailer with the stick. "I think I'll be ordering a couple composite bodies next week. And maybe I should stock up on more components. What do you guys think?"

Though his weary mind was slow to comprehend any subject at the moment, Brent clearly caught that one. He managed a grin. "I think you just might have to do

186

that, Mac. Go for it!"

They were almost at the trailer when a voice called from behind. Hannah Branson was scurrying toward them. "Brent, wait up!"

Brent motioned for the others to continue on. "I'll meet you guys at the trailer," he said as he stopped to wait for her.

Katherine stopped with him. "I would love to meet..."

Martin shook his head from side to side and put his good arm around his sister. "Kath, we need to keep walking."

"Marty, I only..."

He continued to guide her down pit lane. "No. I said we're walking!"

Hannah joined Brent and reached down for his hand. "Congratulations. I think you amazed just about everyone here today."

Brent frowned. "Except for Harris I'll bet."

"Oh, I don't know," she bantered. "He has to be impressed in his own way. He really didn't need the win today, but he would never admit it. With second place here and the Coltons being DQ'd, he now leads the series in points." She smiled her perfect smile. "Oh, and by the way, I heard some witness reported to the officials that it was the Coltons who sabotaged our throttle stops back at Rocky Point. So, you and Harris are both off the hook for that one."

Brent read the innocence in her eyes. The want for frankness was significant. "Thank you for teaming with me in the race. I needed the assistance."

"So did I," she said. "I was falling behind. You helped me. We were hitting them pretty good until I skidded."

Maybe it was the fatigue, maybe the victory, or maybe the warm afternoon sun that took over; Brent didn't know. But he cupped her cheeks in the palms of his hands. "I think I owe you this." Then he kissed her soft lips.

She just smiled. "I told you that up on the grid."

He squeezed her hand softly then let it slip from his grasp. Just then he spotted Kimmie Stimpson, alone, watching them from the distance. She made eye contact with him for just a moment and then lowered her head, turned, and disappeared into the crowd.

He gazed through the scurrying multitude, but she was gone. He couldn't get her look out of his mind.

When he returned to the trailer, Wilbur Sowers of Malta Tires was there, celebrating with Mac and Martin. "I believe you just provided me an acceptable report on our new tire compound for the development boys, Marty," he said. "Thank you."

They shook hands and Martin adjusted the arm sling hunging around the back of his neck. "You can thank Brent for that, Wil. It was all his doing. I still can't believe he ran a double header like that. Maybe I should just get out of his way." He looked down at his arm and shook his head in wonder. "I'm getting too old for this stuff."

Brent slumped onto a stack of mounted tires. The stress of running two races finally took its toll. He felt the energy drain from his legs while his arms just dropped to his lap

Mac wrenched Brent's shoulder playfully and looked up at the group. "When you have a good driver with a good piece of equipment, you have a winning combination...in anyone's book."

Wil chuckled. "And don't forget good tires."

"And a good sponsor," Robert added light-heartedly.

The jesting was barely coherent amidst the explosion of piercing exhausts from the grid. The shifter karts roared out of the pits with scorching, grappling tires.

Brent looked up in time to see Kyle Nash lead the swarm toward Turn 1. His heart pounded within his ribs. "I should have an Avenger out there right now," he joked with a weak smile as his head dropped.

Katherine looked at Suz and shook her head. "I have a feeling I'm about to start worrying all over again."

Glossary of Racing Terms

Apex The point in a turn where the entry ends and the exit begins, usually in the center, but it could be earlier or later depending on the chosen line through the turn.

Axle A rotating shaft on which a wheel or pair of wheels are mounted.

Boxstock A specific class category in kart racing that uses a stock Briggs and Stratton engine, as "out of the box" and allowing only minor modifications.

Caliper The stationary part of a braking system that operates by squeezing friction pads against a rotating disc.

Carburetor A device that supplies a fuel/air mixture to an internal combustion engine.

Chassis The framework of a vehicle, usually metal, excluding the body or running gear.

Chicane An offset and return in a straightaway.

Circlip A snap ring to secure a wrist pin in the piston. (two per piston).

Composite A solid material composed of two or more substances.

Cotter pin A safety pin inserted through a hole in a shaft to prevent components from sliding off.

Crankshaft The main shaft of an engine. It changes rotational energy into compressive energy by driving the piston up and down in the cylinder.

Disc brake rotor The spinning disc of a brake system that operates by the friction of pads pressing against its sides.

Driver fairing A body panel that enhances aerodynamics by moving on-coming air around the driver.

Dyno An apparatus used to measure mechanical force (power).

E.T. Elapsed Time (lap time)

Fairings A variety of body panels intended to enhance aerodynamics and reduce drag.

Fulcrum arm A lever that regulates the amount of fuel in a carburetor by opening and closing a needle valve, a factor in carburetor tuning.

Four cycle (or 4-stroke) An engine having intake and exhaust valves, and whose piston makes 2 up-strokes and 2 down-strokes to complete one cycle. The 4 strokes are Intake, Compression, Power, and Exhaust.

Gear hub An object installed on the axle on which a sprocket or gear is attached.

Gearing set Combinations of engine/axle gears that can be changed for different tracks.

Gusset A plate added to the corners of a frame for reinforcement.

Hundred cc Engine size listed in cubic centimeters. 16.4 cc = 1 cubic inch.

Jobber A small scale wholesaler.

Marque The brand or make of a product.

Monocoque When the body is integral with the chassis.

Nerf bar A safety rail between the front and rear wheels to prevent the invasion of an opponent's wheel.

Piston ring A springy split-metal ring that seals the gap between a piston and the cylinder wall.

Pop-off pressure A setting by an adjustable spring in a 2-cycle carburetor that operates the fulcrum arm, a factor in carburetor tuning.

Spindle Vertical pivoting part of the steering system where the front wheels mount.

Sprint track A racecourse having left and right hand turns, usually ½ mile in length or less.

Struts Braces mounted to the sides of a seat to support the driver's load.

Tachometer (tach) A gauge that shows engine's speed of rotation in revolutions per minute (rpms).

Tie rod A rod that ties the front wheels in alignment. It adjusts steering toe-in and toe-out settings.

Throttle The valve or lever mechanism that regulates the supply of fuel to an engine.

Two cycle (or 2-stroke) An engine that has no valves and whose piston makes 1 up-stroke and 1 down-stroke to complete one cycle. It does this over 10,000 times per minute. The oil and gas are mixed together and combusted.

About the Author

BORN IN THE ROLLING hills of Chambersburg, Pennsylvania, Larry Mellott is a home builder and certified residential building inspector. His construction experience has taken him to Jamaica, Philippines, Ukraine, Brazil, Canada and Trinidad for missionary work. An avid auto enthusiast from youth, he loves MG roadsters and racing karts and Formula Vee sports cars.

He and his wife of 40+ years, Bonnie, raised three children, now with children of their own. When not traveling, they live quietly in their rustic chalet among the evergreen trees of rural south-central PA, enjoying the changing seasons.

Larry writes poetry and freelance articles in trade magazines. See Larry's other books, all available through most on-line booksellers, or from his website:

www.larrymellott.weebly.com

More novels by Larry Mellott

Speedway Summer

When Brent Lockeman prepared his uncle's old racing kart for competition, he realized he was preparing more than just a kart for racing. Not only did he face the challenge of the reigning class champion in the biggest race of the summer…he had to face what he himself was really made of.

Project Orion

Cody Hawkins was an honor roll student, star of the varsity basketball team and an aspiring journalist. But when partnered with a new transfer student to build a dune buggy for competition with a rival school, events spiraled out of control on every level, leaving him to question his own self-assurance.

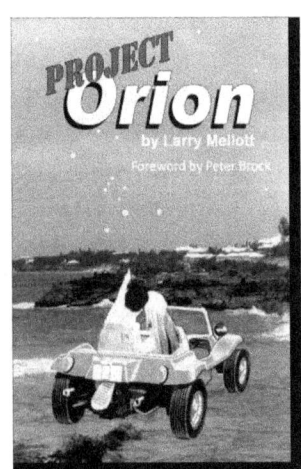

Reconcile

A blackballed Grand Prix driver may be young engineer Russ Thorton's last hope to prove his prototype race car is not the jinx the sports car world has labeled it to be. With everything on the line, he must overcome all that is sacred to him.

mystery on Sandy Islet

When Dylan Porter took on the small remodeling job at a secluded beach house, little did he know about the conspiracy that would engulf him. Just how much could the sheriff, the senator and the sweet young artist next door be involved?

www.ingramcontent.com/pod-product-compliance
Lightning Source LLC
Chambersburg PA
CBHW051510170626
46811CB00002B/733